MW01595996

The Adventure of the Dying Debutante

A New Sherlock Holmes Mystery

Note to Readers:

Your enjoyment of this new Sherlock Holmes mystery will be enhanced by re-reading the original story that inspired this one —

The Adventure of the Dying Detective

It has been appended and may be found in the back portion of this book.

The Adventure of the Dying Debutante

A New Sherlock Holmes Mystery

Craig Stephen Copland

www.SherlockHolmesMystery.com

Copyright © 2021 by Craig Stephen Copland

All rights reserved. No part of this book may be reproduced or transmitted in any form or by any means, electronic or mechanical, including photocopying, recording, or by an information storage and retrieval system – except by a reviewer who may quote brief passages in a review to be printed in a magazine, newspaper, or on the web – without permission in writing from Craig Stephen Copland.

The characters of Sherlock Holmes and Dr. Watson are no longer under copyright, nor is the original story, *The Adventure of the Dying Detective.*

Published by:

Conservative Growth Inc.
3104 30th Avenue, Suite 427
Vernon, British Columbia, Canada
V1T 9M9

Cover design by Rita Toews.

Cover images:

Silhouette of Sherlock Holmes, © Shutterstock under license 19095361

Image of hangman's noose, © Shutterstock under license 1095214682

Image of blond woman in white dress, © Shutterstock under license 648591628

ISBN: 9798510309249

Dedication

To those courageous men and women who served in zones of conflict in their countries' armed forces, who were wounded in ways from which they can never fully recover, and who returned to civilian life, determined to live the best life they possibly could.

If you enjoy this story or if there are ways it could be improved, please help the author and future readers by leaving a constructive review on the site from which you obtained the book. Thank you. Much appreciated,

CSC

Contents

Acknowledgments

All of us who write Sherlock Holmes pastiche mysteries are obligated to express our profound gratitude to Sir Arthur Conan Doyle for his creation of Sherlock Holmes.

So, again, dear ACD, thank you.

As readers of my New Sherlock Holmes Mysteries know, every story in this series is written as a tribute to one of the sixty original stories in The Canon. The one you are about to read was inspired by *The Adventure of the Dying Detective.*

Many of the chapter drafts of this story were shared with the Buenos Aires English Writers Group at our weekly online meetings. Since COVID struck, our loyal members have scattered to all corners of the earth, but once a week we gather electronically to help each other. It is a highlight of our week. My appreciation for their encouragement and friendship is duly noted. Thank you, my friends.

Members of the Vernon Writers Critique Group have also provided valued advice as I wrote this story, as did my weekly writing buddy, Geoff White.

Special thanks goes to Cheryl Adamkiewicz for her generous provision of copy editing and to Miss Linda Lee Holling of Ladyard, Connecticut for allowing me to use name and many aspects of her persona in the story.

All of my stories are reviewed by my wife, Mary Engleking, and my big brother, Dr. James Copland. Their general suggestions and copyediting are invaluable. Again, I thank my loyal beta readers who have reviewed so many of my efforts and made useful suggestions.

I take full responsibility for any and all historic and geographic errors. However, one of the advantages of publishing independently is the ability to correct errors almost overnight. Should readers find them, they are kindly requested to notify me and I will make the required fixes immediately.

CSC (craigstephencopland@gmail.com).

Chapter One

A Visitor After Midnight

 atson, wake up."

I felt the friendly but firm hand of Sherlock Holmes on my shoulder, rocking me awake.

"Wha ... what time is it?" I muttered.

"It has just gone midnight. Please get up and join me in the parlor. We have a visitor."

I bumbled out of my bedclothes and shuffled down the stairs to our front room. As I approached the back of the sofa, the first thing I noticed was the head of exceptionally blond hair, Scandinavian in hue and somewhat disheveled. I walked around until I was looking at the owner.

The woman could not have been much over twenty years of age and was leaning back on the sofa, with her long legs stretched out in front of her. They were covered in what was called a *bicycle skirt,* a long, loose garment that had a row of buttons and holes up the middle of the front and a corresponding row up the back. When riding on a bicycle, adventurous young women fastened the buttons to form two trouser legs. When no longer riding, they re-fastened them to form a single skirt.

Her pale face was perfectly formed, marred only by the dark circles under her eyes. Those eyes were ice blue and blazed as if lit from behind. Her entire appearance indicated a heritage either in Holland or Scandinavia. She stuck me as having the innate ability to make people, men and women alike, stop and stare at her.

"My dear Doctor," said Holmes, "allow me to introduce Lady Giselle Vanderstone of Great Harlaxton Park in St. Albans. She has pedaled here on her bicycle and has some concerns to express to me. Given the hour and the setting, I bowed to discretion and insisted that whatever she had to say must wait until you were present."

I recognized her name straight away. Two years ago, she had come out as a debutante at the Queen Charlotte's Ball and had been hailed in the society pages as the one who caught the eyes of all the eligible bachelors at the event and throughout the London season of that year. It was reported that she had spurned several proposals of marriage by earnest young fellows whom she considered either too poor, too dim-witted or too short.

"Good evening, my lady," I said as I sat down across from her. "And for what reason have we the honor of your visit at this hour?"

She sighed and rolled her eyes ever so slightly. "In case you had not noticed, Doctor, it is no longer the evening. It is Saturday morning. And the reason for my coming to this modest corner of London is to seek the protection of Mr. Sherlock Holmes because members of my miserable family are trying to murder me. And yes, a cup of tea and a glass of decent brandy would be appreciated."

She seemed about to say something more but had a short fit of coughing and covered her mouth with her handkerchief. I could not help but notice her elegant, long fingers and the small fortune in rings that adorned them.

"Tea and brandy coming up," I said and I made my way into our kitchen. It was a holiday weekend in August, and Mrs. Hudson was off visiting family somewhere. So, I would have to prepare the tea myself. As I was leaving the room, Holmes spoke to her.

"You can begin the statement of your case whilst the tea is being prepared. Just speak loudly enough for Dr. Watson to hear you."

"No. I shall wait."

I delivered tea for the three of us, and then Holmes and I waited until she had finished her cup and half her snifter of brandy. She put down her cup and saucer, coughed again, gave the room a disapprovingly visual inspection and began.

"You need to know that because I am young, beautiful, rich and blond, it is usual for men to treat me as less intelligent than they are. I assure you I am not. I speak five languages fluently, play seven instruments well, have visited over twenty capital cities on the Continent, can dance thirty-two different dances, and have read all of the classics."

I allowed myself the unkind thought that the classics had not likely been read in their original Greek or Latin and were perhaps in abridged editions.

"You will be treated with all deserved respect, madam," said Holmes. "Pray continue. Which members of your family do you believe are trying to kill you?"

"It is not a matter of *belief,* Mr. Holmes. It is a matter of certain knowledge. Every member who is currently residing in our London house, with the exception of my brother, is in on it. That includes my step-brother and his wife, my step-sister and her husband and my cousin."

She coughed again and took another sip of her brandy. As she placed the snifter on the side-table, her head nodded as if she were about to fall asleep. The woman was utterly exhausted.

"If you would like," I said to her, "I have a small bottle of medicine that might help your cough."

"I have one already with me, provided by my own doctor, specially formulated for my particular congestion. I do not need anything from you."

"Good to know," said Holmes. "Now then, back to our family of killers. Why would they want you dead?"

"My family is conspiring to kill me so that they can claim the family estate, all the properties in England and beyond, and all the assets and securities. My father was a very wealthy man before he died."

"In whose name is the wealth now held?"

"Mine. I control all of it."

"Indeed? Very well, then please continue. Accusing people of conspiring to commit murder is a serious charge. What evidence do you have to prove your accusation?"

She started to speak, but was overcome by a long yawn. She gave her head a shake and took a deep breath.

"During dinner this evening, the conversation was forced and stilted. I could see suspicious looks being passed between them, especially on the bovine face of my step-sister."

She stopped, coughed again, and took another sip of brandy.

"Madam," said Holmes, "strange looks do not constitute evidence. Surely you—"

"I *know* that. Don't interrupt me and keep listening. I excused myself from the lower floor after dinner as I find their banal banter intolerable, and I went up to my rooms where I could read for the evening. However, I was terribly sleepy and retired early for the night. Immediately before shutting of my lamps, I paid a visit to the lavatory that is attached to my bedroom. It sits on top of the lavatory on the first floor. I overheard my step-sister and sister-in-law chatting. I could not make out every word that they said to each other, but they mumbled for a minute, and then the two of them laughed. I then heard my step-sister say, 'The little bitch will be dead by morning. Won't that be lovely?'"

"You do not, by chance, own any annoying dogs, do you?"

"Two. Both male."

"And the names of those you overheard, please."

"Baron and Prince."

"The women, madam, not the dogs."

"Constance Vanderstone and Estella Baynes."

"Thank you. Carry on."

"I shall. At a quarter past eleven—I had not been sleeping at all after that incident—I heard muffled laugher coming from the main floor. I got out of bed and crawled out of my room so I could not be seen and hid by the edge of the stairs. The entire lot of them were in the front parlor laughing, and I could hear them speaking about how they would divide up the assets of the entire estate once I was, and I quote, 'dead and gone.' Those were the exact words they used, and they were speaking about me."

"By name?"

She coughed yet again and looked as if she were about to collapse on the sofa out of sheer exhaustion.

"If by that you mean were they using the name of Lady Giselle Vanderstone, *no*. When speaking of me behind my back, they invariably refer to me as *Lady Macbeth*, or *Medusa* or, most frequently, *She Who Must Be Obeyed*."

"If they spoke behind your back, how is it you know what they said?"

"Once or twice, I overheard them. On other occasions, my brother heard them and reported to me."

Holmes paused his questions and picked up his pipe. I chided him.

"Tobacco can wait until later," I said and nodded in the direction of our visitor.

He scowled and put the pipe away.

"Very well. I will come by your house at nine this morning and make inquiries."

"I could be dead by then," she said. "If you are as good a detective as they say you are, you would not want to have a client dying on you, would you? And I do not want any of them knowing that I have come to see you. You need to come *now*."

Holmes was clearly not interested in venturing out in the middle of the night based solely on the reports of overheard conversations. I offered a suggestion.

"My lady, permit me to speak to you as a doctor. You are terribly tired and not feeling well. The night air should be avoided. Perhaps it would work best if you were to catch a few hours of sleep here on our sofa. I can wake you up at six o'clock, and we can take you back to your home before any of your family members are awake. They shall be none the wiser, and you will have at least a few hours of rest, which you very much need. Mr. Holmes and I will then stay with you until your concerns are resolved."

She gave me a hard look and then shrugged.

"Fine. Wake me up at six and have a pot of tea waiting. Good night."

With that, she flopped down on the sofa without bothering to take off her boots. By the time I had found a blanket to lay over her, she was sound asleep. Holmes gave me a bit of an annoyed look and retreated to his bedroom.

I returned to my room, crawled back into bed, and lay awake for some time. Twice I heard Lady Giselle coughing, but by half-past one, she had fallen sound asleep. I was relieved. A good night's sleep that *knits up the raveled sleeve of care* is one of the best medicines ever known.

I set my small alarm clock for a quarter-to-six so that I could have time to prepare a pot of tea. I had a few minutes to spare and indulged in half-a-cup myself before organizing a tray for our guest. At six o'clock, I entered the front room, bearing a service of tea and a few scones that had been fresh three days ago but were the best I could find on short notice.

"Good morning," I chirped. "Wake up, young lady. We have an interesting day ahead of us."

There was no response. I called out again, somewhat louder.

She must have been thoroughly exhausted before falling asleep. I put down the tray and gave her firm, athletic shoulder a little shove back and forth.

Her hair covered the side of her face, but her neck seemed oddly colored with a faint bluish hue. The sight alarmed me, and I pulled hard on her shoulder to expose her face.

Her eyes were wide open, staring up at the ceiling. Her lips tinged with blue. She was not breathing.

Immediately, I thrust my hand against her throat to check her pulse. There was none. Her muscles had begun to harden. She was dead.

I gasped and staggered back.

"HOLMES!!!"

Chapter Two

Not a Good Morning

"**H**OLMES!! HOLMES!!" I kept screaming until he appeared, pulling his dressing gown around him as he emerged.

"Good heavens, Watson. What in the—"

I was pointing a trembling hand at the body of Lady Giselle Vanderstone. Holmes was quickly beside me and instinctively placed his hand on her throat.

"Oh, no," he said, barely above a whisper. "How long has she been dead?"

"At least three hours. No more than five. I heard her cough at half-past one. I—"

"But she was fine when she came here, wasn't she? Other than her cough? What could have stricken her?"

I forced my mind back to the brief time passed chatting with her after midnight.

"Holmes, she was not sick. There were no other symptoms ... of anything."

He leaned his face down until his nose was almost touching her mouth and sniffed.

"There is a faint trace of lemon, a citrus scent. Did you give her anything?"

"Only the tea. You and I both drank it. It came from the same canister as I used this morning. There is nothing wrong with it. I had some myself. It was fine."

Holmes reached down to the floor, lifted Lady Vanderstone's handbag to the coffee table and dumped out the contents. An eight-ounce glass bottle holding a yellow liquid and held in place by a stopper immediately caught my eye as it did Holmes's.

I picked it up, undid the stopper and sniffed the opening.

"It's a lemon extract," I said. "Likely mixed with some honey. Good for sore throats and coughs."

I lifted it to my lips to sample a taste.

"DON'T!!" Holmes shouted at me.

I didn't, and I handed it over to him.

He smelled it.

"It's lemon, but there is a faint trace of almond. My guess is that it was adulterated with cyanide."

"Did she ...did she take her own life after talking to us?" I said, horrified.

"Did she strike you as someone about to do such a thing?" asked Holmes.

"No."

"Nor me. Our guest has been murdered. Please cover her. I need to contact the police straight away."

As I pulled the blanket up over the lovely face and blond hair, Holmes rushed down the stairs and out to the pavement of Baker Street. I heard him blow on his police whistle. Five minutes later, he came back into the room.

"A constable came. I sent him running down to Marylebone to the telephone box to call Scotland Yard. I expect an inspector and a few constables will arrive soon."

We hurried to prepare ourselves for the day and, once washed and dressed, we sat in silence, waiting for the police.

We did not have to wait long. At a quarter-to-seven, I heard carriages pull up to the curb and walked over to the bay window to see who had arrived.

The first man to step out of the smaller carriage was the aging but still sallow-faced Inspector Lestrade. I hustled down the stairs to let him in.

"Good morning, Inspector," I said as they entered. "A bit of a surprise to see a senior man working the night shift of a holiday weekend."

Lestrade harrumphed, pushed on past me and spoke back over his shoulder as he climbed the stairs, holding the railing as he made his way up.

"We old boys don't mind taking the holiday shift. Lets our younger men have a bit of time with their families. And getting a call to a murder at 221B Baker Street, well, it just does not get any more interesting than that, now does it?"

The inspector examined the body on the sofa briefly and sat down, his pencil and notebook at the ready.

"Right then, Holmes," said Lestrade. "Tell me all about it. How is it that a murder took place right under the nose of the great detective, Mr. Sherlock Holmes?"

I could tell that Holmes was stifling a sharp response, but he composed himself and gave a detailed account of everything we had been told by Her Ladyship, who now lay dead on the sofa a few feet away from us.

"From what you've told me," said Lestrade, "it looks like she was not imagining things when she said someone was out to kill her. If she came straight from her home to here, then it stands to reason that it was one of her family. What do you say to that, Holmes?"

"I agree, or possibly her doctor."

"Right. But doctors do not normally like murdering their regular fee-paying patients. Bad for business. Right, Dr. Watson?"

I grunted my agreement.

"Well then, Holmes, as it has not yet gone seven o'clock and therefore not likely that the members of said family are up and around, it being a Saturday morning, I suggest we go and pay them a visit. Not far from here, is it? Spring a little wake-me-up surprise on them, shall we? You two, me and six constables. What do you say to that, Holmes?"

"Six constables? Where can you round them up so quickly?"

"They're sitting in the growler behind my carriage. When I announced at our headquarters that we had a murder at 221B Baker Street and it took place in front of Sherlock Holmes, every man in the room jumped up and volunteered to come with me. Six was all I could fit in. Brought my most senior men. A spot of reward for their years of service. Seems my lads find you more interesting than locking up drunkards and pimps."

Once in the Scotland Yard carriage and on our way to the Vanderstone family's London house by Primrose Hill, Lestrade pumped Holmes and me for any additional data we had about Lady Giselle and her family. I recounted what I remembered about her from reading the society pages, and Holmes added some pertinent details from his prodigious memory.

"The mother," said Holmes, "the first Lady Vanderstone died in childbirth after the birth of her daughter."

"The one who is now dead on your sofa?" said Lestrade.

"Precisely. His second wife, Lady Margaret Vanderstone, died five years ago of consumption."

"Or so," I said, "it was reported in the press. The medical establishment knew otherwise."

"And what did they know?" asked Holmes.

"She was certainly not well and was indeed suffering from consumption, but she had become terribly saddened by her condition and took her own life. She hanged herself. That information was withheld from the public for the sake of the Lord Vanderstone and his family."

"How very thoughtful of our doctors," said Holmes. "However, the cause of His Lordship's death was well known. He died in a riding outing three months ago. There was an inquest, as he was an accomplished horseman, but the verdict was a tragic accident."

"So, who did that leave?" asked Lestrade.

"The son, an older brother to Giselle. After Cambridge, he was an actor for a very brief time and then joined the BEF. His regiment was sent to the war in the Cape Province. A year after he arrived, his unit was attacked, and he and ten of his men died."

"But Holmes," I said, "she said she spoke with her brother last night.

"Then she must have a second brother I was not aware of. Regardless, the estate, which must be worth well over a million pounds, all went to the daughter."

"According to her," said Lestrade.

"An excellent point, Inspector," said Holmes. "Yes, according to her. It would be useful to review the will to confirm that claim."

"Where did the money come from? He wasn't one of the old landed nobility, was he?"

"No. He was of the newly moneyed set and came by his wealth during his own lifetime. All made, so I have read, from trade between England, Africa and the Americas. All legitimate, or as much so as any of that business ever is."

"And now, who does it all go to?"

"That will be for the courts to decide unless the other family members agree amiably on a division of the assets."

"Which is what she told you they were talking about."

"Correct again, Inspector."

Our two carriages cut off Baker Street and on to the Outer Circle of Regent's Park. The sun had been up for nearly an hour, but on a

Saturday morning of the August Bank Holiday weekend, the citizens of London were not. In the brisk morning air, we hurried along the roads that were empty except for the occasional chap out walking his dog.

The London house of the Vanderstone clan was just off Avenue Road and backed on to the open fields and copses of Primrose Hill. It was one of the largest houses in London, built a century ago by some duke whose descendants decided twenty years ago that they would rather live in Mayfair along with their cousins and sold it to Reece Vanderstone.

A high brick wall and a wide gate made of black iron marked the perimeter of the grounds. The tops of the vertical bars of the gate were shaped into spear tips and painted gold. The gate was closed, but a sleepy-eyed young sentry opened it when he heard the name of Scotland Yard.

The mansion sat back nearly a hundred feet from the gate, and the grounds surrounding it were perfectly landscaped with stately trees, ornamental shrubs and garden beds. The summer flowers had faded and been replaced with several hundred chrysanthemums in various hues. In the early morning sunlight, the property exuded refined taste and orderly wealth.

We pulled up to the entry portico, and another young man came stumbling from behind the house, his bootlaces not done up and tucking his shirt into his trousers as he limped toward us.

"Are you the groom?" asked Inspector Lestrade.

"Aye, that I am."

"Got you up out of bed, did we?"

"My day starts at eight. The gatekeeper has a bell chord he pulls if'n anyone gets here early. I'll take your horses if'n you wants them looked after whilst you're here."

I took a close look at him. He had raven-black hair and pale skin and a black patch over one eye. The other side of his face was badly scarred. His posture, however, was erect, and he walked with his shoulders back and his chin up. He had 'veteran of the battlefield' written all over him, and I thought I'd have a brief word with him.

"Looks like you got a bit beat up. Back from the Cape?"

"Aye. Not the life I'd hoped for but happy to be alive."

"Same way I felt when I came back from Afghanistan twenty-five years ago. So, I can tell you, it gets better. Just keep trudging on and don't give up. You'll make it."

He gave me a warm, knowing smile such as can only be exchanged between wounded veterans, and I gave him my card.

"Decent of you, sir," he said and then read my card. "Dr. Watson? You the same as writes all those stories about Sherlock Holmes?"

"I am indeed, and that's Sherlock Holmes himself walking toward the front door. I'm afraid we have a spot of business to clear up here."

"Why? What's happened? I'm sorry, sir. It's not my place to ask, but did something happen to one of the family?"

He appeared to be visibly upset, and I gave myself a kick for not keeping mum about the reason for our visit.

"Nothing for sure yet," I lied. "I'll let you know later, once it is all settled."

I gave him a clap on his shoulder and hurried to join the others. They were standing at the door and had already knocked, but no one had appeared to open it.

As we were standing there, a woman pedaled up on her bicycle, dismounted and joined us under the portico.

"Good morning, gentlemen," she said. "Is there something with which I can help you?"

She was a petite woman of about the same age as Holmes and me. She was dressed in a dark blue skirt and jacket and a cream-colored blouse and struck me as the sort of woman one might expect to meet in an office in the City.

"Scotland Yard, madam," said Lestrade. "Just a bit of police business to sort out, nothing to worry about. Mind telling me who you are and why you're here so early on a Saturday morning?"

She did not immediately reply and gave Lestrade a good looking over before answering.

"My name is Holling, Miss Linda Holling. I am the secretary of the Vanderstone estate, and I arrive at this hour every Saturday morning so I can have some peace and quiet as I try to sort out the family affairs."

"I assume," said Holmes, "that there are some complications following the death of Lord Reece Vanderstone."

Again, she did not answer straight away and gave Holmes an even more thorough visual inspection than she had given Lestrade.

"Who are you?"

"My name is Sherlock Holmes, madam, and I am assisting Scotland Yard in this matter."

"I've heard about you. And what I've heard tells me that this is not just a little bit of police business, is it? And you have six constables with you. What's going on?"

"We will make that known once we have all the members of the family together. If you have a key to the door, would you be so kind as to open it and let us in?"

She gave Lestrade a wary eyeball and opened the door.

"I'll let you in. The butler has the holiday weekend off," she said.

Lestrade then turned to her.

"Madam, do you live far from here?"

"No. I live in St. John's Wood. Why do you ask?"

"Were you present in this house last evening?"

"No, I departed at dinner time and returned to my home. Why are you asking?"

"Madam, we are indeed here on a serious matter. As you were not present last night, I suggest you return to your home as it will not be possible for you to carry on with your business this morning. Please give your address to one of the constables. It is quite likely that we will come by before the end of the day to ask you a few questions."

"Very well. I expect I shall be far more forthcoming in answering your questions than you have been in answering mine."

We left her chatting with one of the constables, and the rest of our entourage stepped inside.

"Doesn't look like anyone is up and around yet," said Lestrade. "That's a bit of all right. Spread out, men. Knock everyone up and tell them to meet in the dining room. Don't worry about the servants' rooms. Just the family members. And then block off all the doors so that nothing and no one goes in or out. No deliveries in. Don't even let the trash be taken out. Right, men, hop to it."

LONDON 1887

Chapter Three

The Vanderstones of Primrose Hill

Unlike most of the London homes of noble families, the walls of this house were not covered with portraits of long-dead ancestors. In their place were paintings by the recent collection of aesthetes and several large canvases showing scenes from Africa. Corners of the rooms and the top surfaces of furniture were adorned with carved statues from the Dark Continent, and no less than four of the recently imported Benin bronze heads. Someone, most likely the recently departed Lord Reece Vanderstone, must have traveled to the tropics several times in the past.

Fifteen minutes later, five thoroughly annoyed members of the Vanderstone family sat around the table in the dining room. The two couples were still in their bedclothes and dressing gowns, and one fellow, sitting somewhat away from the others, was casually dressed as if he was about to go for a morning walk through nearby Regent's Park.

Inspector Lestrade introduced himself, Holmes and me and then took a seat at the table, leaving the constables standing around the circumference of the room.

Lestrade continued. "Ladies and gentlemen, I am terribly sorry to have to barge in on you like this—"

"You bloody well should be," said the largest of the three men facing Lestrade. "Now, either explain yourself immediately or get out."

The fellow who spoke was large and athletically endowed. He looked the type who might have made an excellent number four or five in the engine room of a crew of heavy eights scull.

The woman who was part of the other couple sneezed and blew her nose into her handkerchief, not entirely silently. Her husband— I assumed that was the relation to her of the gaunt red-haired man beside her—gave her a condescending look and then rolled his eyes toward the ceiling.

"We are conducting an investigation of a crime," said Lestrade, "and we will not be leaving until we have finished it. And furthermore, neither will any of you."

"Don't be ridiculous," said the sturdy oarsman. "In case you are not aware of it, our wives have demanding responsibilities with one of England's leading charities, and my brother-in-law and I hold senior positions in the City at the Bank of London and South America. We will not be kept away from them whilst you do whatever you do when conducting your ... what did you call it?... your *in-ves-tig-ation*. Is that understood?"

"Is that so?" replied Lestrade. "Well now, in case *you* were not aware of it, sir, today is Saturday, and your offices are closed. Tomorrow is Sunday, and they will still be closed. And the next day is the August Bank Holiday, and so they will still be closed. And if we are not finished our work by Tuesday, well, this house has a telephone, and I am sure your office does as well. You can call in and give your underlings whatever instructions they need and receive same from your superiors. If you attempt to leave the grounds, you will be physically restrained by one or more of the constables. Is that understood?"

He received silent glares in return. However, I did notice one of the constables winking at his nearest colleague and a quick small smirk. Holmes was sitting silently, observing every posture adjustment and eye movement of the lot of them.

"Right," said Lestrade, "now that we have that settled, I'm going to go over my list of who you all are. We can start with you, Mr. Senior-in-the-City. Says here that you are Mr. Bentley Baynes, and the lady beside you, your wife, is Mrs. Estella Baynes and she was the stepdaughter of Lord Reece Vanderstone. Is that correct, sir?"

"It is, and are you going to explain why you have invaded our home or not?"

"I'm getting to that. Right, now, you sir, the gentleman with the red hair. Are you Mr. Jefferson Vanderstone, step-son of his now-departed lordship? And the lady beside you is your wife, Mrs. Constance Vanderstone. Is that right?"

"It is, Copper. Yes."

"You will address me as Inspector Lestrade. Thank you."

"I shall call you whatever I jolly well want to, and if you don't like it you can jolly well arrest me. Thank you, *Inspector* Copper."

A bemused smile appeared on Lestrade's face. "If you can count, sir, you might notice that there are six *coppers* standing behind me and they are prepared to do whatever I ask them. Isn't that so, lads?" He turned around in his chair and nodded to the row of constables.

They answered with a chorus of "Yes, sir. Right you are, sir. Ready, aye ready" and similar affirmations, all voiced cheerfully.

"And you, sir," he said, looking at the younger fellow who was sitting somewhat by himself. "It says your name is Cuthbert Molesworth. It's not clear to me where you fit in, so how about you explain that to me."

"I am a cousin to the Vanderstone family," he replied.

"A cousin? Families have scores of cousins. Try to be more specific."

He bowed ever so slightly. "I am the *sole* first cousin to the family. Lord Basil Vanderstone had only one sibling, my mother. His first wife, Lady Ruth Vanderstone, had none. I was an only child. Therefore, I am the sole first cousin. Is that a sufficient explanation, sir?"

"Right. That helps. So, Mr. Baynes says that he and his brother-in-law are important men in the City. He didn't include you. What do you do, Mr. Molesworth?"

"I am a writer, an author, and I must say it is an unexpected honor to be at a meeting attended by one of England's most popular authors, Dr. John Watson. A delight to meet you, sir. I have read all of your wonderful stories."

He smiled and bowed slightly in my direction, and I nodded back.

"Now then," said Lestrade, "is that the entire lot of you who were in the house since last evening?"

"You left out Giselle," said Mrs. Constance Vanderstone, followed by another sneeze.

"Giselle? Who's Giselle?" asked Lestrade, his face all innocence.

"Our sister," said her husband. "She's asleep up in her rooms. Your six coppers must have missed that end of the hall."

"Did they, now? Well no, Mr. Vanderstone, they did not. They entered that room, and there is no Giselle there."

I noticed as I knew Holmes did as well, a few involuntary looks of confusion and several sets of eyeballs glancing around at each other

"Then where in the blazes is she?" demanded Baynes. "She left all of us right after dinner last night and went to her room and she hasn't appeared since."

"Lady Giselle Vanderstone," said Lestrade, "is currently at another location, where she is dead."

Gasps and verbal sputters followed his announcement. I glanced at Holmes and noticed his careful observation of their reactions.

"Yes, she is dead and we believe she was murdered. And since all of you were amongst the last to see her alive, that makes all of you suspects. We regret the inconvenience, but we are conducting a murder investigation. Therefore, we will speak to all of you individually, and you may not carry on conversations between each other, except between husbands and wives, until we say it is all right to do so."

He then turned to Holmes. "Anything else to add, Mr. Holmes?"

"Where is Lady Vanderstone's brother? We need to speak to him too."

"That won't be possible," said Jefferson Vanderstone.

"Why not?"

"Because he is six feet under the earth in the family plot in St. Alban's."

"I was referring to her second brother."

"There is no such person. There was only Clayton. He was a captain in the Coldstream Guards, and he was killed on duty in the Cape."

Chapter Four

Not Welcome in the Dining Room

olmes said nothing in reply and nodded toward Lestrade.

"Right. You are now dismissed to your rooms. No one may leave the property," Lestrade ordered.

"I have plans to see my daughter at her school," said Mrs. Baynes. "She is looking forward to a holiday weekend with her mother. It would be beastly of you not to allow her that opportunity."

"Schools are still on their summer term," said Lestrade. "If she has not seen you all summer, she will not be devastated by missing you for a few more days."

"Are we permitted to enjoy our breakfast," asked Mrs. Vanderstone, "or would that interfere with your investigation?"

"A constable will be present at the table," said Lestrade. "Now, please return to your rooms or the library or the back lawn or wherever you wish. We shall call each of you when we need to have a chat."

Mr. Cuthbert Molesworth strode immediately over to me. "Dr. Watson, it is such an honor to meet you. I can only dream of someday being as successful an author as you are. Would it be too much to ask you to take a look at a few pages of my latest effort?

Your expert opinion would be invaluable to a young writer just starting out."

"More than happy to," I said, "but under the circumstances, best to wait until this nasty business is over and done with. Perhaps you can drop by next week sometime. I'm sure you know the address."

"I do indeed. The second-best known address in all of London, after Buckingham Palace, of course."

"Of course."

After they had all departed, Holmes turned to Lestrade.

"My dear Inspector, kindly clarify. Are you engaging my services on this case or not?"

"I don't have to. You said that Lady Giselle Vanderstone already did."

"Might I remind you, she is dead."

"But some contracts survive death, war, flood, change of government and even devastating defeats of the English national rugby team by a ragtag team of scrawny Welshmen. You can send your account to her estate, which you say is worth millions. I have no doubt they will pay you eventually."

"Will they now? Very well then, whom shall we interrogate first."

"I'll leave that to you, Holmes. Whomsoever you want. I might find it interesting to watch you."

"Are you quite sure that your men can carry out a thorough search of the house?

"They've searched a hundred or more crime scenes each."

"Brilliant. Then let us start with the stable boy. Most likely, he will be in his room out in the mews. Mind you, he was lurking in the hallway and eavesdropping whilst we were in the dining room."

"Was he now?" asked Lestrade. "Fine, but why him?"

"Grooms and maids always know things. Have him meet with us in the parlor."

A few minutes later, the young lad we had met when we arrived limped into the front room, accompanied by a burly constable. I could see that he was awfully ill at ease and stepped over to meet him.

"At ease, soldier," I said. "Nothing to worry about. A few questions, that's all. Just a formality. Come, sit down and tell Mr. Holmes whatever he wants to know."

He took a seat on one of the sofas and leaned his cane against the front of it. I sat down beside him.

"State your name, please, young man," said Holmes.

"I ... I'm ... my name is Othniel Clarke. Tha ... that's Clarke with an 'e,' sir."

"Thank you. You already know why we are here, don't you? No, no, don't shake your head. You learned why whilst listening in the hallway."

The poor fellow blushed. The scars on his face caused an uneven distribution of the reddish hue, with streaks of white interlaced with blotches of red.

"Yes, sir. Yes. I heard about it."

"Excellent. Then we shall not have to waste time telling you. We can start by your telling us about yourself. How long have you worked here?"

"Since June, sir. I started this year, 1902, on the fifteenth of June."

"And how came you by this position? Did Lord Vanderstone hire you?"

"No … no, sir. His Lordship had perished just a few days before. I ... I came here because I had served under Captain Vanderstone, his Lordship's son. He was my captain, sir. In the war. The war in the Cape, sir."

"Where he died?"

"Yes, sir."

"Were you there when that took place?"

"Yes, sir. I was."

"Tell me what happened."

The poor fellow's eyes were already reddened, and his hand began to shake.

"Holmes," I said, "is that entirely necessary? The last thing any soldier wants to recall is the day his unit was destroyed, and all his mates were killed."

"It's ... it's all right, Doctor. Thank you," said Clarke. "I can do it. Captain and ten of us were sent forward to scout out the enemy. We made camp for the night where we thought we'd be safe. And we weren't. After it got dark, those Boers ambushed us. Shot volleys and shells into our shack and set it alight. All my mates died along with our captain."

"But you survived. How?"

"I was on my way out to go to the latrine when the shots and shells hit. I took one in the leg and got burned up, but I crawled to the latrine and hid. They didn't find me."

"You were lucky."

"Not so sure of that. If'n I'd died, I'd be a hero instead of an ugly cripple. I believed I was doing it all for England. Fat lot of good that did me."

I put my hand on his shoulder. "You are a hero, Othniel. You served your country bravely. Don't let anyone ever tell you otherwise."

"Quite so, Doctor," said Holmes. "Now then, how did you get this position? You weren't in a cavalry unit. What do you know about horses?"

"After I came home and was let out of the hospital, I couldn't find work anywhere. A man can't live on what little pension they give someone who only served for a few months and came back in a basket. My captain, that would be Captain Vanderstone, had mentioned his younger sister quite a few times. Seemed he was close to her, and I thought I would come and tell her I served with her brother and that she might think I was a decent fellow and give me some work. Well, I did that, and she hired me straight away. It was the week after her father had died, and she said she needed all the help she could get. She gave me a job and a roof over my head when no one else would. I thank God for her every night and a dozen times on Sunday. I do, sir."

His body started to tremble and he dropped his face into his hands. I placed my hand on his back and gave the poor fellow a friendly rub.

"There, there, soldier," I said. "Take a deep breath and carry on."

"Yes," said Holmes, "do carry on and tell me what you were doing yesterday evening from supper time on."

"I took my supper in the kitchen with the cooks. I gives them a bit of cupboard love and it makes them laugh, and they give me my supper with them. Right good to me, they are. After that, I waited in my room in the stable case'n any of the family wanted to go out, but they didn't, so about ten I went to sleep."

"Do any of them usually go out in the evening?"

"Sometimes, if they're here on the weekends, but last night they just all sat in the library and played cards. At least that's what the cooks said they were doing. I wouldn't know for sure."

"When do you last see Lady Giselle?"

"Just before supper, sir. She came out for a walk over the back lawn and up the hill."

"Was she alone?"

"No, sir. There was an older chap with her. I believe he was her doctor."

"And was that the last you saw of her?"

"Aye, it was, sir."

Holmes and Lestrade thanked the young fellow, and I walked back with him to the door and gave him a few more words of encouragement.

"Who are you going to call for next?" I asked Holmes

"Would you mind, Inspector," he said to Lestrade, "asking your men if they have had an opportunity yet to inspect Lady Giselle's room. If they have, did they find the name of her doctor?"

Chapter Five

Doctor Quacksalver

ive minutes later, we were in Lestrade's police carriage and on our way to Harley Street.

"It won't hurt to leave the lot of them for an hour," said Lestrade. "They're all sitting around the dining table playing some new game of cards. Two of my men are sitting with them and noting everything they say. Unless they're speaking in some secret code, they won't be able to pass anything significant between them."

Dr. Garrett Anderson's surgery was on Harley Street, just south of Marylebone and appeared to be every bit as prosperous as the other medical establishments on the same block. It was just after eight when we knocked on his door and were greeted by an attractive dark-skinned woman in a nurse's uniform.

"I am very, very sorry, gentlemen, but if you do not have an appointment, you cannot come in. The doctor is a very, very busy man."

"Scotland Yard," said Lestrade as he pushed in past her, "is even busier. Give our apologies to any patients if we cause them to be kept waiting longer than usual. Kindly tell the good doctor to meet with us straight away."

We entered the finely appointed waiting room of Dr. Anderson. The furniture was all in the most recent style as could be supplied by Harrods, and the walls were covered either with paintings showing serene pastoral and lake scenes. Plaques with wording that began, *Dr. Anderson says,* and followed by some gem of commonsense health practice filled all remaining space.

A display rack in the corner was packed with copies of a book, *The Consumption Conqueror: Garrett Anderson's Miraculous Recovery from Certain Death to God-given Fine Health.* Perched at the top of the rack was a large, framed photograph of the author, looking somewhat froggish with large eyeglasses and a face that lacked a firm chin. Clearly, the man did not want anyone to underestimate his heroic stature.

There were two patients waiting to see him. Had Sherlock Holmes been asked to describe them, he most likely would have said that they were *Three 'C' Ladies*—church, charities and cats.

After waiting for five minutes, Lestrade was about to barge into the doctor's inner sanctum when he emerged, accompanied by a third female patient, this one much younger. He gave us a pained look.

"If this is not particularly important, and I assume it is not, then I see no reason you cannot return later this afternoon once all my patients have been treated."

"Well, it is particularly important," said Lestrade, moving toward the door of the examination room as he spoke. Holmes and I followed him in, trailed by the doctor and his unmistakable mutters of indignation.

Once inside, Lestrade held out the bottle of yellow liquid.

"Did you provide this medicine to Lady Giselle Vanderstone?"

"I most certainly did."

"What's in it?"

"The contents are secret. They are my own discovery and a patent has been applied for."

"Are they now? Well, there are no secrets when a crime has been committed. So, you can either tell me now, or you can come with me to Scotland Yard and tell me there."

The doctor affected a face of righteous indignation. "What crime!? The medicines I provide are utterly legal. Regardless of what the press go on about, there is no crime in creating a medicine whose ingredients cost a few shillings and selling it for a few pounds. That is just sound business. Lady Vanderstone was more than happy to pay for it and would have paid twice as much. You can ask her yourself."

"That's not going to be possible, doctor," said Lestrade, "seeing as how she is dead."

This time, the expression on the doctor's face was of involuntary shock.

"Dead? No. She was fine when she came here yesterday morning. What happened?"

"What happened was that she took a swallow of your secret elixir and promptly died."

"That's...that's impossible! There is nothing whatsoever in my *Congestion Conqueror* mixture that could do anyone any harm. Impossible! Whatever befell her could not have been from my medications."

"Is that so? Then best you prove it and write out what you put in this bottle, and we'll decide if it was lethal or not."

Dr. Anderson moved slowly and deliberately over to his desk and sat down. He took out a pad of paper and wrote a list. When finished, he made a point of reviewing it carefully several times before returning to Lestrade and handing it to him. He handed it on to me and Holmes. The list of ingredients was quite predictable. There was an abundance of lemon juice, a tablespoon of honey, three dashes of narcotics, and few spices and a generous base of Yellow Chartreuse liqueur. No wonder it was a popular treatment regardless of its results.

"Thank you, Dr. Anderson," said Lestrade. "Now, you say that Lady Vanderstone got this from you yesterday morning. Was that the last time you saw her?"

"Yes."

"Was it now? Well then, how is it that a witness says he saw you with her up on Primrose Hill late yesterday afternoon?"

He looked nonplussed but only for a second. "You asked when was the last time I *saw* her. When a doctor *sees* a patient, it is generally understood to mean he *saw* her, that is *examined* her in his surgery. I paid a visit to her later that day, but I did not *see* her in the medical sense."

"Is that so? And whilst you were not *seeing her* whilst strolling along beside her, did she imbibe any of your ... what did you call it ... your *Constipation Conqueror*?"

"My *Congestion Conqueror*? Yes, she did. Twice. Once at the start of our exercise and once again when we finished, just before she went in for supper with the other members of her family. It was highly efficacious and helped her considerably."

"Who held on to the bottle of elixir during that time?"

"I did, and I left it with her when I departed. What has that to do with what happened to her?"

"It would seem, Doctor, that at some time between her bidding you good day and her death after midnight, someone infused her bottle of Chartreuse, honey, and lemon with cyanide."

The man's eyes widened, and he looked honestly horrified. "If what you say is correct, it must have been poisoned after I departed."

"Unless you did it."

"How dare you. Don't be a fool. She was under my care. I acted diligently and conscientiously to keep her in good health, as I do with all of my patients. Acting in any other way would be a complete abrogation of my medical responsibilities."

"Well then, did she have any enemies that you know of?" asked Lestrade.

The doctor closed his eyes, brought his hands together in front of his chest and took several slow, deep breaths before responding. Having calmed himself down, he answered.

"Yes. Her entire family. She despised every one of them, and they hated her."

"Why?"

"Why what? Why she despised them or why they hated her?"

"She is now dead, and they are not. So, it is more important to know why *they* hated *her*."

"They were not my patients, and therefore I can only tell you what she told me."

"You can start there," said Lestrade.

"She said that they were jealous of her beauty, her ability to attract wealthy suitors, and the closeness of her relationship with her father. After the death of her brother in the war, she was her father's only true child. The others were his step-children, and he was never particularly fond of them."

"So *she* said."

"That is what I already told you. Were you not listening?"

Lestrade ignored the jibe and continued. "Did she identify any one of them who might have been more antagonistic toward her than the others?"

"No. They all hated her in equal measure."

"Well, thank you for that. Doesn't help narrow down the suspects much, but thank you all the same. We'll let you get back to your clients but have to tell you, for now, not to leave London."

As Lestrade turned to depart, Holmes put his hand on his arm and then looked at the doctor.

"One more question, if we may, Doctor. Lady Giselle referred several times to her brother. However, her only immediate brother was killed in the Cape. Do you have any insights into whom she might have been speaking of?"

"What did she say about him?"

"That she trusted him."

"It certainly was not Jefferson Vanderstone, her step-brother. The words she had for him would cut glass. Maybe her cousin."

"Cuthbert Molesworth?" asked Holmes.

"If that's his name. But I only say that because she disliked him the least. Now, if you will allow me to wish you a good day, I must get back to my patients."

Once back in the police carriage, Lestrade asked Holmes and me for our opinion of Dr. Anderson.

"Assuming," said Holmes, "that he has a firm alibi for his time after he bade good day to Miss Giselle, we can likely strike him off our list or at least move him down to the bottom of it."

"I agree," said Lestrade. "What about you, Dr. Watson?"

"I do not believe him to be a murderer. Mind you, I do not believe him to be a doctor either."

"Is that so?" said Lestrade. "Care to elucidate? He had his certificates on the wall, did he not?"

"That he did," I said. "He took his medical training at the Imperial College of Medical Sciences but not at the Imperial College of Medicine."

"What's the difference?"

"The second is located here in London. The first is in Calcutta. You too can become a doctor through their program for a hundred pounds. Shall I get a certificate for you?"

Chapter Six

We All Hated Her

"Take charge, Holmes," said Inspector Lestrade once we had returned to the Vanderstone's London house. Which one of them shall I have my lads bring in next?"

"Mr. and Mrs. Jefferson and Constance Vanderstone, if you would please. They appear to hold the top place in family rank even if not in volume."

A constable soon ushered the chosen couple into the parlor. Now that he was standing, Jefferson Vanderstone's height was remarkable. He was quite a bit taller than Holmes, and had he been standing straight instead of hunched over, he might have been in excess of six-and-a-half feet. His receding reddish hair and thin face added to his severe appearance. His wife, on the other hand, was not thin, and she dabbed her nose with her handkerchief as she assumed her seat in one of the chairs Lestrade had set out.

Mr. Vanderstone pulled up an additional chair and placed it in front of the one he intended to sit in. Once seated, he stretched out his long legs and put his feet up on the vacant chair. His finely tooled shoes were gleaming.

"I do hope," said Mrs. Vanderstone, "that this will not take long. Thanks to your holding us against our will, we were taken away from enjoying quite a fun new card game together. Are you familiar with *Royal Auction Bridge,* Mr. Holmes?"

"No."

"No? Well then, you really must learn how to play it. So much more engaging than whist. And here I thought that famous detectives were up on all the latest social advances. But perhaps it is a factor of your age, Mr. Holmes."

"No doubt you are correct. I do have a curmudgeonly disdain for the latest mindless frivolity. However, we are not here to discuss my ways of wasting time; we are conducting an investigation into a murder. But as you have mentioned your game of cards, please tell me who won the game last night."

"Cuthbert, by quite a margin."

"What was his best hand?"

"He bid six no-trump—we thought he was daft—and then he won the round. He is quite the sharpie."

"If that makes him one, then I suppose he is. Very well, enough of the card game. Allow me to continue by asking you where you were from eight o'clock last evening until eleven o'clock. Ladies first, Mrs. Vanderstone."

"We were all in the library playing cards. The five of us. We started immediately after dessert and port and continued to midnight. And we had such a good time, didn't we, darling?"

This last question was directed to her husband, who then took over command of the conversation.

"We most certainly did, my dear. Except for the occasional minute when one or the other of us had to answer a call of nature—and none of us traveled beyond the ground floor lavatory to do so—we never departed from the room. Therefore, I suggest, Mr. Holmes, that you and your friend, the inspector, consider looking at those with whom Giselle may have met after she departed the house and went wherever it was she went to go and die. She had a singular ability to engender hatred toward her from everyone she met, within minutes."

"I shall assume," said Holmes, "that you were amongst those from whom she elicited hatred. Is that correct?"

For a second, there was no response as the two of them looked at each other. Mrs. Vanderstone shrugged and answered.

"Entirely correct. There is no point in denying it. We all hated her."

"And why, madam, did you, and I mean you specifically, hate her."

"Because she attempted to destroy our marriage by seducing my husband."

"Really, darling," said the husband, "we don't have to air—"

"We are being interrogated by Scotland Yard, my dear. We have nothing to hide, and it is to your credit that you withstood her wiles and resisted her advances. I am very proud of you. You—"

"All right, you told the truth. You do not have to go into detail."

"We may," said Holmes, "ask for more details later. For now, permit me to suggest that one of the reasons everyone in the family hated her was that she was the primary recipient of her father's estate, and the rest of you were left with a handful of farthings by comparison. Is that not correct?"

"Absolutely not," said Jefferson Vanderstone. "The estate was divided fairly by my stepfather. Giselle, Estelle and I each inherited the same amount. A generous bequest was made to Father's favorite charities, and substantial sums were given to those members of the household staff who had served the family for years."

Holmes did not immediately respond. What we had just been told was at odds with what Giselle Vanderstone had said to us prior to her death.

"Are those terms," asked Holmes, "laid out in your father's will?"

"They most certainly are. You may see for yourself if you pay a visit to the family solicitor. In fact, there is a copy in the library. Go and look and disabuse yourself of any thought that we were envious of her being treated as the favored child. Reece Vanderstone, may his soul rest in peace. treated his blood offspring and his step-children fairly and equally."

Again, Holmes paused his questions as he absorbed the contradictory data he had been given. His doing so gave Mrs. Vanderstone an opportunity to fill the void with her thoughts.

"In case it had not occurred to you. Mr. Holmes, much as we were not terribly grieved by the news of her death, none of us had either the motive or the opportunity to get rid of Giselle. It would appear that you are merely a dog who is barking up the wrong tree."

"Is that what dogs do when they detect the scent of another dog on a tree? If so, then would you mind asking your cousin, Mr. Molesworth, to come and have a chat with us."

Chapter Seven

Please, Bring the Maid

Mr. Cuthbert Molesworth entered the room, smiled cheerfully at Holmes, Lestrade and me and sat down.

Holmes eyed him for a moment and then asked him, "Where were you, and what were you doing last evening from the time you were served dessert until eleven o'clock?"

"I was in the library with the Vanderstones and the Bayneses. We had a marvelous game of Royal Auction Bridge. Kept it going until midnight."

"And were all five of you there throughout the entire evening?"

"Entirely. Well, if you must know, except for the occasional departure I had to make to use the lavatory. The same goes for the others, but we all used the one on the ground floor and returned immediately. Didn't want to lose a minute more from the game."

"Who won the game?"

"I did."

"What was your best hand of the evening?"

"I bid six no-trump and won the hand. Quite a bold move, if I do say so myself. Helped me take the pot into my pocket. We were only playing for farthings, mind you. But it gives a chap a right good feeling to win over his rich relatives, if you know what I mean, sir."

"I do, and are you going to do as well from your share of the estate? Or will the rich relatives take it all?"

"I'll do all right, I guess. Uncle Reece was a fair man, and he divided everything up quite decent like."

"And what was the division? Do you know?"

"We all know, sir. It's in the will. He left ten percent to charity, twenty percent to the Vanderstones and the same to the Bayneses. Giselle would have received thirty as she was the only true child and not a step-child. I was given fifteen, and the rest was disbursed amongst longstanding members of his staff and friends. We all did quite all right by him."

"Much more than you would have received from your writing."

"Oh, yes, sir. Much more. I can afford now to move out of my shared flat in Soho and into a cozy set of rooms in Knightsbridge. Like I said, sir, we all did well, and we all agreed it was fair and square."

Holmes paused and then asked another question.

"What is the name of the maid who was here last evening?"

Mr. Molesworth was not expecting that question nor, for that matter, were Lestrade or I. He looked understandably confused and unsure of himself but answered all the same.

"Umm...Gladys. Yes, that's it. Gladys. Miss Gladys Fealy. At least I assume she was *Miss*. I've never heard anyone speak of her husband. Frankly, I can't imagine who would want to marry her. Mind if I ask why you want to know that, sir?"

"Because I have changed my mind and wish to speak to her next. Mr. Molesworth, would you mind accompanying one of the constables up to her room and asking her to come down? We were informed that her normal Saturday morning shift begins at eleven o'clock, and it is almost that time now."

"If that is your wish, Mr. Holmes, I shall do so. Happy to be of whatever assistance I can be."

As soon as he had departed the parlor, accompanied by a constable, Lestrade asked.

"Why the maid, Holmes? She had nothing to gain from the death of Lady Giselle."

"Precisely and therefore nothing to hide."

"Right. Then you believe the others are hiding something?" said Lestrade.

"They obviously colluded on their accounts of last night all the way to the visits to the lavatory. I am hoping that the maid will give an independent rendering of the evening."

"But why would they be hiding anything? We can read the will, but there does not appear to be any motive to do in Lady Giselle. They're all getting their piece of a very large estate. You seem to suspect them of something, but what could be their motive?"

"At this precise moment, my dear inspector, I do not know. I only know that what they have told us so far bears the smell of having been concocted. That is why we need to speak to the maid before any of them have access to her."

Two minutes later, I was startled by a cacophony of voices coming from the dining room. It was followed immediately by the entrance of the constable to the parlor. The look on his face said that something was amiss and rather badly.

"The maid, Inspector, sir, is dead."

Chapter Eight

Sniffed to Death

I leapt up from my chair and hurried toward the staircase. Holmes was right behind me, followed somewhat more slowly by Inspector Lestrade.

Cuthbert Molesworth must have announced the news to the card players at the same time as the constable did to us. Mr. Baynes was ahead of us on the stairs and bounding up to the servants' quarters on the top floor.

By the time I entered the room, Bentley Baynes was already leaning over the body, slapping her face and shaking her.

"Don't touch her!" I ordered.

He glared at me, uttered a nasty oath and shouted back. "She is my maid in my house. Do not tell me what to do."

"I am a doctor. Stand back and let me attend to her."

That instruction was met with another oath and a disparaging comment toward the medical profession. Fortunately, Inspector Lestrade and Holmes had appeared, and the inspector bellowed as if he were a sergeant-major on the parade square.

"By order of Scotland Yard, get away from her!"

"You have no authority here. Go and fetch me a glass of brandy!" came the reply from Baynes.

"Constables, remove this man from the room. If he resists, you can handcuff him to the radiator in the kitchen."

Feeling two sets of strong hands on his shoulders, Baynes stood up, shuffled out of the room and stood outside in the hallway whilst I examined the body in the bed. She was a woman of African origin and rather on the large side. "She has been dead for at least twelve hours," I told Holmes and Lestrade. "There are no obvious signs of injury or of having been placed in the bed by someone else."

I was overheard by the cluster of family members who were now crowded into the doorway.

"She was overweight," called out one of the women. "She drank far too much, and she must have had a heart attack."

Her verdict was followed by words and murmurs of agreement.

"Constables!" ordered Lestrade. "Escort the family members back to the dining room and close the door behind you."

Once we were alone, Holmes and Lestrade began an immediate inspection of the room, and I carefully examined the body of Miss Gladys Fealy.

"Right," said Lestrade, "I don't see any bottle of anything interesting. No wine or spirits, no laudanum, no miracle elixirs from Dr. Anderson. What about you, Holmes?"

"There is a drawer with her personal papers in it that we can examine later. However, we must begin with the assumption that she died of natural causes. What are your initial thoughts on that, Watson?"

"She is of the age and body size where the stopping of her heart would not be surprising. But there are some items I suggest you two take a look at."

"Pray tell," said Holmes.

"She has a mop cap on her head."

"So she does," said Holmes. "I would be surprised if she did not. I cannot imagine women of her age and station going to bed without something to keep their hair in place. Why do you mention it?"

"It's on the wrong way."

"What, backwards?" asked Holmes.

"No. Sideways."

"Interesting," said Holmes. "And your second observation?"

"Her fingernails."

"What of them?"

"I cannot tell without examination under a microscope, but there is a substance under several of them that looks a lot like small particles of skin mixed with a minuscule amount of blood."

"Excellent, Watson. Perhaps acquired whilst fighting off an attacker?"

"Perhaps. Now, take a look ... better still, smell these. They were lying on the bed under the edge of her thigh."

I handed him two small glass vials whose tops had been broken off and popped open. He held one up to his nose and sniffed.

"Amyl nitrate," he said. "It is commonly prescribed by doctors for relief of angina and other heart problems, is it not?"

"Yes. It increases the heart rate and the flow of blood throughout the body. Her use of it suggests that she may well have had a heart condition."

"Which supports the suggestion that she died of heart failure," said Holmes.

"Yes, but ... it also produces a short-lived euphoric effect. Similar to your past habit of using cocaine but much safer even if the achieved results do not last as long."

"Then why are you bringing it to my attention?"

"Because there are two empty vials, not just one. They were found together and have similar amounts of residue in them. They appear to have been opened and used simultaneously. The effects of one vial are more than enough to improve the circulation, even with repeated inhalations for an hour or more."

Holmes looked at me quite intensely and then at the broken vials. "Are you suggesting, Watson, that two people used them at the same time and enjoyed the euphoric feelings together?"

"It is a possibility," I said.

Chapter Nine

A Suspicious Death

"Are you two," said Lestrade, "getting around to telling me that this death looks suspicious? Or did she just sniff herself to death?"

"A bizarre cause is always possible until proven otherwise," said Holmes, "but the most probable possibility is foul play."

"Right. And what killed her? Making her heart happier? Took a friendly sniff and had a heart attack? Those little glass vials are murder weapons? See how far that will get you in a courtroom."

For several seconds, Holmes sat in silence, gazing at the plump dead body in the bed.

"I suspect that her head is resting on the murder weapon."

Lestrade gave Holmes a hard look and then walked over to the bed, gently lifted the head of the deceased, and slid the long pillow out from under it. He flipped it over and examined the pillow case. Holmes joined him and pulled his glass from his pocket. The magnification was not necessary. In the middle of the pillowcase, I observed a small stain, faint but definite.

"Water by itself," said Holmes, "would have dried up without leaving any marks. Whilst saliva consists almost entirely of water,

45

it also contains mucous and trace elements of several chemicals. These cause a stain to be left behind. I suggest, Inspector, that this woman was pleasantly drugged and then suffocated with the pillow. Dr. Watson has suggested that the materials he noticed under her fingernails could be particles of skin and blood. Is Scotland Yard's laboratory capable of identifying skin, blood and saliva?"

"They've come a long way in the past few years and could likely do so, though I doubt it would stand up in court unless bolstered by other evidence. Scratches on their necks, perhaps. But you've given me enough to rule this a suspicious death, declare this a crime scene and have the body taken to the laboratory."

Lestrade sent a couple of his constables through the house and the grounds to find the family members and bring them to the dining room. Ten minutes later, we were again facing the five relatives of Giselle Vanderstone, all of whom were looking at us as if they had been weaned on a pickle. They were muttering amongst themselves and shifting their bodies in their chairs and their hands on the table in a manner calculated to exhibit umbrage and impatience.

"As a matter of courtesy," Lestrade said to everyone and no one, "I am informing you that I have called for the unit of the Metropolitan Police to come here immediately and remove Mrs. Fealy's body and have it taken to the police morgue for examination."

His announcement was met with a moment of silence followed by Bentley Baynes's noisy rising to his feet and pointing a finger at Lestrade.

"Bloody hell you will. You will do no such thing! You have no legal right to remove a body that died from natural causes from a private home, and you know you don't. If you dare violate English law and do that, I will have you up in front of a magistrate faster that you can hop in and out of your coppers' chariot. Which, looking at you, is not all that fast."

His little cut at Lestrade's age brought about a round of smirks and chuckles from the other members, except for Cuthbert Molesworth, who maintained a blank face.

The inspector had every right to take offense but showed none. A serene, smug smile flickered across his face, much as does the face of the man holding a Royal Flush when his opponent with his four aces lays his cards down and prematurely reaches for the pot.

"Mr. Baynes," Lestrade began, "you are utterly correct, and I commend you on your knowledge of English law. The police have no right to remove a body after a doctor has pronounced a person dead. And we would never even think of doing so ... unless we had serious reason to believe that the deceased was a victim of foul play. It so happens that I have considerable and justifiable reason to believe that Mrs. Fealy was murdered."

The room became utterly silent.

Those seated around the table then began to exchange glances. Mrs. Vanderstone and Mr. Molesworth both began to say something and stopped. Finally, Mrs. Baynes spoke up.

"Inspector, your conclusion is nonsense. The woman was at least seven stone overweight, was not young, and could not climb a flight of stairs without having to stop and catch her breath. For her heart to fail as she slept is entirely to be expected."

"Madam," said Lestrade, "may I remind you that I was already aware of everything you have just said. She was certainly a candidate for heart failure. Had there been no other evidence to suggest that her death was anything but from natural causes, I would not dream of calling in our coroners and specialists. I do not take such actions lightly. That I am doing so should be reason enough for you and the other members of the family to conclude that there is justification for my actions."

Again, another minute of silence.

"Then you should tell us what that evidence is," said Bentley Baynes.

"No, sir, I should not. Such evidence is preliminary at this time. It may or may not be revealed as the investigation proceeds. I regret that that is the best answer I can give you today and, sir, you will just have to live with it. Furthermore, you will all have to remain here until we conclude the investigation now of two murders. That is all for now. You are free to leave and continue your card games or strolls or whatever you want to do, subject to the restrictions you have been given."

For a minute, no one moved. Lestrade came over to Holmes and quietly asked, "Who next? The Vanderstones?"

"Not yet. First, we complete the chat with the cousin. Please have one of your lads bring Cuthbert Molesworth back in."

Chapter Ten

Where There Is a Will

"**I** thought you might like to see this," said Molesworth as he entered the parlor. He had a document in his hand that he gave to Holmes and then sat down.

"Your uncle's will?" asked Holmes.

"That it is. I expect you will find it interesting."

Holmes flipped quickly through the first few pages and then concentrated on the remaining ones. When he was finished, he handed it on to Lestrade, who then passed it over to me. The paragraphs dealing with the division of the assets of the estate were precisely what Molesworth had recounted to us. Lord Vanderstone was abundantly fair in his bequests to his children, step-children and nephew.

"If," asked Holmes, "there was no animosity to Giselle arising from the allocation of the bequests, why then did Mr. and Mrs. Vanderstone and Mr. and Mrs. Baynes hate her so intensely?"

"Some reasons should be obvious," replied Cuthbert. "She was a decade younger, much better looking, and was the favorite of her father, particularly after the tragic death of her brother in the war. Then, of course, there were some rather specific reasons."

"Explain, please."

"To begin with, she seduced her stepsister's husband, and Estelle took offense."

"Is that so, or was it Jefferson Vanderstone?"

"Probably both. I would not put it past her."

"Seduced or merely tempted?"

"Can anyone ever know? Bentley says *tempted,* Giselle—privately, of course—bragged to me that she had seduced him. You decide where the truth lies. I fear it is beyond me."

"What then of her step-brother and his wife, Mr. and Mrs. Vanderstone?"

"Giselle despised Constance and was forever ridiculing her about her allergies, sneezing and runny nose."

"Such behavior is nasty but hardly unusual or unknown amongst members of an extended family. It is hardly sufficient to invoke obvious pleasure on hearing of her death."

"Well, there was also the matter of Constance's little dog."

"What of it?"

"Constance adored the yappy little cur and Giselle killed it. Or, to be fair, I should say that Giselle had it taken into the veterinarian and put down. In Giselle's defense, I should note that she did so only after the dog had made yet another indiscretion on the carpet in her bedroom."

"That would give her some reason for not liking her, I suppose," said Holmes.

"That, and the fact that they all believe Giselle was responsible for the death of Lord Vanderstone," said Molesworth.

Holmes paused his questions, took his cigarette case out of his pocket, extracted one and slowly lit it. He inhaled and blew out a long, slow stream of smoke.

"That, sir, is a serious accusation. Kindly explain."

"There's not much to explain. Uncle Reece and Giselle regularly went for an afternoon ride across the Hill. On the afternoon he died, the two of them were out, and Giselle came back to the stable alone. When the groom asked where His Lordship was, she acted shocked that he was not right behind her. She dismounted and walked back into the house, quite unconcerned. The groom waited for a few minutes, and when His Lordship's horse came back without its rider, the groom got up on his horse and went to check on him. He found him lying beside a stone wall, with his shoulder and leg broken and a huge bump on his head. By the time the groom galloped back and found help to come and rescue the old chap, he had died."

"And that was Giselle's fault?"

"We'll never know, will we, sir. But if you were out riding with your father, would you not notice for twenty minutes that he was no longer riding with you?"

Holmes declined to answer, took another long draft on his cigarette and thanked Cuthbert Molesworth for his time and candid answers.

As he was departing the room, he turned back to us. "There was one more thing you probably should know."

"Go ahead," said Holmes.

"Jefferson and Estelle also held Giselle responsible for their mother's death."

"Do you mean that she somehow drove her stepmother to commit suicide?"

"Oh no, not that at all," said Molesworth. "They are convinced that Giselle murdered her. They believe that she slipped a rope around Lady Margaret's neck, strung her up, and hanged her."

"Do they have any grounds, any evidence for believing that?" asked Holmes.

Molesworth shrugged. "Who knows? You'll have to ask them. Have a good day, gentlemen."

With that, he departed, leaving the three of us looking at each other.

"Inspector," said Holmes, turning to Lestrade, "we shall have to leave that one for a later time. Would you mind having one of your men ask Mr. and Mrs. Baynes to come in?"

Two minutes later, the delegated constable returned to the room.

"Begging your pardon Inspector, sir, and gentlemen, but Mr. Baynes told me to tell you his reply and, well, it was not what you might call respectful, Inspector."

"Right, well, out with it. What did he say? His exact words."

The constable looked somewhat flustered and took a deep breath.

"He said that he was having his lunch and you could bloody well wait until he was finished, and he might be available to come in an hour but only after his dessert and port. If you didn't like it, you could take your interview and ... well, you can imagine where he said you could put it, Inspector, sir."

"Right, well you can take two constables with you and grab him—"

"Perhaps," interrupted Holmes, "my dear Inspector, you might reconsider before sending your lads to do that."

"Why would I do that? Scotland Yard does not tolerate such impudence when we are conducting a murder investigation. He should never be allowed to get away with that type of disrespect."

"You are entirely correct, Inspector, and that is precisely why we should allow him to think that he has gotten away with it and triumphed over us. There is nothing so useful as a suspect who has become overconfident. I suggest we leave him to stew in his cocksure juices for an hour before bringing him in—hoisted and carried in at that time, if necessary."

"A bit of the old cat and mouse, eh, Holmes? Is that what you're doing?"

"I suppose you could call it that. Anyway, there is another matter to which I would now like to turn my attention."

"And that would be?"

"This account of the death of the father. I suggest that whilst the family is having its lunch, we should have the groom saddle up three horses and go for a ride. Would that appeal to you?"

"No. You and Watson go. Riding is no longer my favorite pastime."

"If you cannot join us, might you let us have one of your men in your place?"

"Right, take Constable Axline. He can eat when you're done."

He nodded to the constable who had recently been the bearer of the abusive reply. He, Holmes and I then made our way out of the house and to the stables behind it. The constable sidled up to me and whispered in my ear.

"What is he wanting to do on a horse?"

"I haven't the foggiest idea," I said.

.

Chapter Eleven

He Flies Through the Air

"**S**oldier!" I shouted into the stable. "We are in need of your services!"

Othniel Clarke emerged from the stable and gave the three of us a strange look.

"Yes, Doctor. How can I help you?"

"The family members are having their lunch, and whilst they are doing so, Mr. Holmes and I thought we might go for a pleasant ride. Would you mind saddling up three of your finest mounts for us? Three that have some life and spirit to them."

"I ... I can do that if that's what you're wantin', Doctor. Do ... do you want me to come with you, like to be your guide and all?"

"Thank you, no. Constable Axline here says he knows the layout of Primrose Hill and the park. We'll be fine."

"Constable," said Holmes as we waited for Othniel, the groom, to saddle up three horses, "do you have a police revolver on your person."

"Well, no sir. We don't carry them when making calls such as this."

"Are there any in the growler that brought you here?"

"Well, yes sir. There's several."

"Would you be so kind as to run and fetch one whilst the horses are being readied?"

The constable looked at me, and I shrugged. I shared his bewilderment, but I gestured toward the path around the house, and he ran off to get a gun.

I spoke quietly to Holmes. "Are you sure you know how to ride a horse like the ones you asked him to bring?"

"I rode some magnificent mounts during my brief time in Arabia. I shall manage. What about you?"

"I had to learn years ago during my basic training with the Northumberland Fusiliers. Mind you, that was a long time ago."

"It's like riding a bicycle," said Holmes. "You never forget."

By the time Constable Axline returned, Othniel had emerged from the stable with three magnificent horses. One had a gleaming coat that was entirely black and was of similar size as the splendid horse I wrote about years ago, *Silver Blaze*. The second was a dun mare, and the third a large chestnut thoroughbred.

"Was one of these by chance," asked Holmes, "the one Lord Vanderstone was riding on the day he died?"

"Aye, sir. He was on the black, *Starless Midnight*. 'Twas the master's favorite, sir."

"Was it? Well then, I'll take that one."

"Hold on tight," I told Holmes. "That horse won the Grand National a few years back. Isn't that right, Othniel?"

"Aye, that's him. His Lordship charged an arm and a leg for stud fees. He's a busy old boy, he is. Aren't you there, big fellow?"

He gave the horse and friendly pat and sent us on our way.

"Constable," said Holmes once the three of us had trotted off the back of the Vanderstone property and into the open expanse of Primrose Hill, "Do you happen to know where up ahead Reece Vanderstone had his accident?"

"I do. Not far ahead. There's a low stone wall that's left over from when this was still farm land. You'll see it in a minute."

See it we did. The sections of it that were still standing intact were just over three feet high. It went on for over a hundred yards, and the fastest way to deal with it was to have your horse jump if it was capable of doing so

"Wait here," said Holmes.

"Where are you going?" I said.

"To have a good run and a jump."

With that, he gave Starless Midnight a kick and took off in a hard gallop directly toward the wall.

"Doctor!" gasped Constable Axline, "what's he doing? He could kill himself."

The big black horse was thundering directly toward the wall, moving like a tremendous machine. Holmes was riding surprisingly well, but the horse was not slowing down as it galloped toward the stone wall.

"Holmes!" I screamed at him. "Be careful. He'll try to jump—"

At precisely the right instant, the magnificent thoroughbred surged upward, its front legs extended and cleared the stone wall with at least three feet to spare. It landed without missing a stride and galloped on. Holmes reined it in and, having cantered down to the end of the wall, came trotting back to us. He bore the shining morning face of a schoolboy and was positively grinning.

"Utterly exhilarating, Watson. Utterly splendid. No wonder His Lordship loved his daily ride. Did you want to give it a try on your mount?

"No."

"Quite understandable. Well then, I enjoyed it so much that I shall do it again."

"Holmes, really. Have you gone mad?"

"Possibly, but there is method in my madness. Now then, Watson, I need for you to dismount and stand against the wall just to the left of where I went over it. Constable, take the reins of Watson's horse and trot into the copse of trees over to the right. Hide somewhat so that you cannot be seen but so that you can see me as I approach the wall on my second run. When I am ten yards from the wall. You will fire your revolver into the air. Is that understood?"

"Sir, that's a terribly dangerous thing to do. If the horse is startled, you could be thrown."

"Precisely. Now, off you go, both of you."

The constable again looked at me, shaking his head.

"Has he lost his mind?" he asked me as we trotted down toward the wall. "Is he always like this?"

"No, not *always*."

When the constable and I were in place, I gave a shout to Holmes, and he waved back. Then he spurred his horse into a gallop and came thundering toward the wall. At the ten-yard mark, the air was shattered by the loud retort of a gun, and the galloping animal suddenly jolted its body to the right. The inertia carried it forward and it fell over, landing on its side and rolling over. As it fell, Holmes cried out and was thrown directly toward the stone wall. My heart stopped beating, and I lurched forward in an instinctive attempt to catch stop him from crashing into the barricade.

I could not stop him, but his trajectory was high enough that his head, shoulders and all but his left foot cleared the top of the wall, and he went sailing past me, somersaulting into a crumpled heap several yards on the far side of the wall.

I struggled to get over the wall to see if he was hurt. Constable Axline came rushing out of the trees and vaulted over the wall and, in a flash, was at Holmes's side helping him up.

"Good heavens, Holmes!" I shouted, "You could have been killed."

He stood up, wiped his hands off with his handkerchief and dusted off his sleeves and knees. "Precisely. However, a single test is not sufficient as evidence. We need to repeat the experiment. Please return to the copse and Constable Axline, be ready again with your gun."

He got back up on the horse, trotted around the end of the wall and then back a hundred feet from it. Once again, he galloped his steed toward the wall. A second time, the gun went off just as horse and rider were preparing to leap into the air, and the frightened animal jerked its thousand-pound body to the side. This time Holmes was ready and managed to jump off the horse and land on his feet. He controlled his forward momentum and stopped just before running into the wall.

He was grinning and seemed pleased as punch with himself. "Ah, wasn't that capital! Come now. End of riding excursion. Back to our interviews."

If there was ever any justice in the relationship between man and beast, it was exhibited that afternoon when the black thoroughbred kept stepping back every time Holmes attempted to mount him from then on.

The constable and I rode back to the stable and Holmes walked, Starless Midnight trotting along several yards behind him and snorting from time to time.

Chapter Twelve

Sensible with Good Taste

"How was your ride?" asked Lestrade. "You look like you bit the dust."

"I prefer to believe that I flew through the air with the greatest of ease," said Holmes. "However, I concede that your description of the event is somewhat more accurate."

"Right, well wipe the smirk off your face and tell me what happened."

Holmes recited the details of our riding excursion without drawing any conclusions from his experiment.

"Right," said Lestrade. "And I suppose you now have evidence that when a horse is spooked, its rider is in danger of being thrown. That is not overly helpful."

"Lord Vanderstone," said Holmes, "was an experienced rider and took that horse over that wall at least twice a week for the past two years. Those facts were raised at the inquest, but there was no evidence that anyone or anything other than bad luck was responsible. Had they called Starless Midnight as a witness, they might have decided otherwise."

"And now Sherlock Holmes is suggesting that the decision of the inquest was wrong and that someone may have deliberately spooked the horse."

"I will consider it to be a distinct possibility until proven otherwise."

"Right, so who did it?"

"It may well be that Lady Giselle Vanderstone had a hand in it."

"Your dead client?"

"Precisely."

"Well, lucky for you she's dead, or you would likely lose your account with her straight away after saying something like that."

"That is an unusual perspective, Inspector, but far be it for me to quibble with you."

"I agree. All right then, who are you going to drag in here next? The Bayneses?"

"No. It is time for lunch."

"Fat chance of having this lot give us anything," said Lestrade.

"Quite so, Inspector. Therefore, we shall take ourselves out to one of the cafés on Avenue Road. We shall eat quickly and pay a visit to St. John's Wood. It is time to chat with Miss Holling."

"Her? What for? She had no interest in the murders. She wasn't even here."

"People in her position know things."

It was a lovely day in late August and we walked out to Avenue Road and ate a quick lunch. I would have enjoyed more time in the sunshine, but Holmes was in a hurry and he hustled Lestrade and me across the road and into St. John's Wood.

Miss Linda Holling's home was a respectable terraced house off of Acacia Road and gave the impression of orderly but not ostentatious care. We were greeted at the door by a maid who led us into the parlor.

"Please be seated, gentlemen," she said. "Miss Holling has been expecting you. We are very sorry to hear about the passing of Lady Vanderstone. Tea?"

We declined the offer and during our brief wait I could not help but notice the vases of flowers and the interesting paintings that complemented the room. Holmes was also looking around.

"A woman," he said, "of independent means and good taste. An excellent choice of character to recruit to manage a large estate."

He seemed ready to say more, but Miss Holling entered, walked past the three of us and sat in one of the chairs facing us. Two cats came out of some corner of the room and curled up at her feet. With her back straight and her hands in her lap, she looked directly at Lestrade.

"Good afternoon, Inspector. Now is there something with which I can help you?"

"Yes, there is, and we thank you for your cooperation. We have some questions for you."

"Concerning the murder last night in 221B Baker Street of Lady Vanderstone, no doubt."

"Right, and how about you start by telling us how you already knew about it. No information has been released to anyone yet."

"You told me to go and talk with one of your constables, Inspector. He was a fine young man and turned out to be terribly chatty."

"Right, well, we'll have to do something about that. All right then, Holmes, lay on with your questions."

"Thank you, Inspector," said Holmes. "Now then, Miss Holling, when we met you at the door this morning, you informed us that you are the manager of the Vanderstone estate. Is that correct?"

"It was, Mr. Holmes. Of course, after what took place last night, I may or may not have the same position tomorrow."

"Of course, thank you. And how long have you served in that position?"

"Three years and three months."

"And before that, what did you do?"

"I was an Administrator in the Admiralty for twenty years, and prior to that I taught school."

"How came you to your current position?"

"His Lordship's wife had recently died. She had quite capably helped him manage his affairs, and he needed someone to replace her."

"But how did he come by you?"

"The Vanderstone businesses had numerous engagements with the Royal Navy, and I was involved in the transactions. He offered me my current position at a salary nearly twice what I was being paid and I accepted."

"Ah, well, he and you must have got along well for him to do that."

"Not at all. He considered me—his words—difficult and demanding, picky, penny-pinching and parsimonious, illiberal and ill-tempered and overly orthodox. Therefore, he knew I would be the ideal person for the job."

"I assume," said Holmes, "that his affairs included having to deal with his children and step-children."

"They did."

"And did those dealings usually go well?"

"No."

"Could you please be more explicit? What was the nature of your interactions with them?"

"Telling them *no*."

"With regards to their demands for more money?"

"Yes."

"But His Lordship was not exactly short of cash, was he?"

"Never."

"Ah yes, he was an exceptionally wealthy man. And you, I assume, would be the ideal person to tell us the value of his estate," said Holmes.

"Do you mean his personal estate or the value of the firm?"

"The firm, madam?"

"The Fidelity and Empire Trading and Investments Company Limited."

"What does that firm do?" asked Holmes.

"Since it was established shortly after the death of his wife, it has carried out almost all of His Lordship's business transactions and held his assets."

"Why would he want to do that through a firm instead of directly?"

"His fear of—his words—those scurrilous scalawag socialists and radicals."

"Madam?"

"He was worried that the socialists, who are growing in power with each passing day, might be elected and form the government. They would immediately increase the Estate Duty from the current eight percent to over twenty percent on all forms of wealth and on the passing of inherited wealth after death. He was loath to let that happen and therefore moved all of his assets into the firm believing that it would continue on independently after his death."

"How very astute. What then was the remaining value of his personal estate?"

"About one thousand pounds."

"Madam, that seems impossible. His property in St. Albans and this property are worth many times that amount. The stables and horses alone are worth more than that."

"He sold all his land and chattel to his firm for one pound."

Can he do that legally?" asked Holmes, looking at Lestrade and me as if we could provide an answer. Both of us shrugged our ignorance.

"That, Mr. Holmes," said Miss Holling, "is what expensive lawyers are paid for."

"Were the assets and shares of the firm included in the bequests in his will."

"No. The transfers of the shares are covered under separate corporate covenants."

"How very astute," said Holmes. "And did you assist him in making these arrangements?"

"No, they had been completed immediately prior to his engaging my services."

"But after the death of his wife?"

"Yes."

"From what you said a moment ago about his needing help from his wife to manage his affairs, I am surprised that he was able to carry out all that was necessary by himself. Was he assisted by a solicitor? By an accountant?"

"By both, but primarily by his daughter."

"Lady Giselle Vanderstone?"

"Yes. Up until the time she took it upon herself to die on your sofa, she had a brilliant head for numbers and for the affairs of industry and commerce. She orchestrated the establishing of the firm. It was quite the undertaking given its complex nature and value."

"I am sure it was. Very well then, what is the approximate value of the firm?"

"One million, seven hundred and fifty thousand pounds, give or take."

I gasped. "He is one of the richest men in the Empire."

"No, Doctor," said Miss Holling. "He *was*."

"What happened to his shares after his death?" asked Holmes.

"The Articles included a clause stating that in the event he was incapacitated, which would include his becoming dead, there was a proxy in place giving the voting rights to his son and daughter. On the death of Clayton, a similar proxy gave the voting rights to his sister, Giselle."

"Would that have given control of the majority of the shares to Giselle?"

"It would. The shares held by the other members of the family were only twenty-five percent. She controlled seventy-five. And therefore, she could have the firm do whatever she wanted it to do."

"Did that become a problem? She did not strike me as likely to require it to make poor decisions."

"She had recently passed a motion appointing herself as the general manager and requiring the firm to pay her a salary."

"That is not entirely unreasonable," said Holmes. "How much was she to be paid?"

"Two hundred and fifty thousand pounds a year."

Again, I gasped. "Why that is more that the highest-paid owners of the largest firms in England are paid. That is beyond belief."

"If that had gone ahead," said Holmes, "would not the firm have been drained of all of its assets within a few years, with everything being transferred over to her?"

"It would. It was a rather brilliant scheme," said Miss Holling. "The other members of the family were not pleased."

"Because," said Holmes, "their shares would become increasingly worthless. Is that correct?"

"Yes."

I interrupted here with some questions of my own.

"But why would she do that? She was already one of the richest young women in the country? What more could she have wanted?"

Miss Holling smiled at me, somewhat condescendingly. "My dear Doctor, once you pass beyond the vice of greed, you arrive at the vice of power. It is highly addictive, without mercy, and it had her in its thrall."

"Merciful heavens, why every one of them, all five, had reason to want her dead."

"Yes Doctor, they did. And they joked about ways of getting rid of her numerous times. I overheard them at least three times. I can only assume that they finally succeeded. Now, if that is all, gentlemen, kindly excuse me as I have some necessary work to do with respect to my immediate and uncertain future."

"Before we leave, madam," said Holmes, "there is one other conundrum with which I hope you can help us."

"If I can, I will. What?"

"When we met with Lady Giselle, she referred several times to her brother. However, she was not referring to Captain Clayton Vanderstone. He was dead. Do you have any suggestion to whom she was referring?"

"The groom, Othniel Clarke. But she did not call him *her brother,* she would have called him *her brother's.*" She pronounced the possessive noun with a drawn-out emphasis on the *zzzz* at the end of the word.

"Please explain, madam."

"The groom, Othniel, served under her brother in the war in the Cape. Giselle thought the name Othniel was too elevated for him, and she always referred to him as *my brother's man.* Doing so reduced his status to that of a servant. After a few weeks, she shortened it—degraded it would be more like it— to *brother's.* I suppose that was better than calling him *Burnt Face* or *One-eye.* That was what the rest of the family called him."

"Why, of all the people in the household, would she trust *him*?"

"Because she could not diminish him any farther than he was. He was already a pathetic wreck of a man, and he was at her beck and command like an obedient puppy dog. She tossed him whatever scraps that she had leftover, and he wagged his tale and wanted to please her. He was loyal, and no one else was."

Chapter Thirteen

Trashed

"May I suggest," said Holmes once we had returned to the Vanderstone home, "that we not reveal that we have had a chat with Miss Holling."

"Makes sense," said Lestrade. "Right, then who do you want next? The only ones left are the Bayneses. Shall I have them brought in?"

"No, not yet. We should allow them a little more time to twist in the wind. Have your men completed their search of the premises? Perhaps we could have them let us know what they found."

Two seasoned men in uniform met us in the library. Spread out on the desk and various tables were books, papers, personal effects, trash, and articles of clothing. Constable Axline—he who was quite a good rider—delivered his report.

"We have completed our search of the premises, Inspector, sir," he said, "and we took note of the following. The two couples, the Bayneses and the Vanderstones, obviously do not live in this house and were making a temporary visit and participating in a meeting. Their items of clothing, shoes, personal effects, toiletries, books to read and the like are quite limited. Enough for a few days but no more. However, they did bring quite a few files and cases of letters and such, indicating that they were expecting to be in some sort of business meeting. We have laid out a few of those items for you to see, but there are more still up in the bedrooms."

Holmes and Lestrade got up and quickly perused the papers and files, nodded, murmured and sat back down. It struck me that there was a paucity of files related to the firm and the estate. The constable, of course, would have been quite selective. But any family business and firm that carried on as much business as this family did should have produced a much higher volume of critical documents. Inspector Lestrade, however, was clearly not concerned.

"Well done, my lads," said Lestrade. "Carry on."

"Nothing to report about the trash," said Axline. "Only what might be expected after a dinner. They had lambchops, so the bones were in the trash. But the dinner must have been tasty as there were hardly any food scraps left over. A newspaper and the dinner place-name cards were in with the kitchen waste. There were some personal items in the waste baskets from the lavatory, of course, and some crumpled notepaper in the bedrooms and the library, but there was nothing of significance written on them. And then there were two more newspapers that may have been left behind in the parlor and cleaned up by the maid in the evening. But that was all."

"Which newspapers?" asked Holmes.

"Both the *Times* and the *Manchester Guardian*, sir. I guess they had to cover both the Liberals and the Conservatives. Oh, there was a *Financial Times* as well, sir. That was in Mr. Molesworth's room."

"Thank you," said Holmes. "Pray continue."

"Well sir, things got a little more interesting in what was not in the trash in the lavatories. Mrs. Constance Vanderstone had an elixir bottle from that same doctor as gave one to Lady Giselle Vanderstone. We heard you and the Inspector talking about it over at Baker Street, and Constable Aduddell spotted the same name on another bottle. This one was labeled *The Allergy Alleviator*. We thought you might want to know that."

"Well done," said Holmes. "Most commendable skills of memory as well as observation."

"Thank you, sir. Let me move on to what they were reading as I thought it might be telling. Mr. and Mrs. Vanderstone were reading a book each by Mr. Dickens and Jane Austen. The Bayneses brought along Lord Bulwer-Lytton and one of the *Brontë sisters' novels. Mr. Molesworth had a copy of one of your books, Dr. Watson—all about Mr. Sherlock Holmes. That all seemed more or less the usual, but then there was Lady Giselle's room. It was a bit peculiar.*"

"*In what way, Constable?*" asked Holmes.

"*Her ladyship lived here, so she had many more books than the visitors, of course. Well, sir, I recognized them. You see, I have a sister. She lives with the missus and me, and I love her dearly, but she's a spinster and quite taken with the suffragettes. And she reads all the same books.*"

"*Does she? Go on.*"

"*I made a list of them, sir.* There was *Lady Audley's Secret, Armadale, East Lynne, The Awakening, Carmilla, Sweeney Todd, The Great God Pan, She* and one of Dr. Watson's stories, the one about that nasty chap named Milverton. Do you know those books, sir?"

"I am quite familiar with the authentic account of Charles Augustus Milverton, and therefore I have not bothered to read the good doctor's account. I am not familiar with the others, but perhaps Doctor Watson is."

I was indeed and said so. They all were stories of women who asserted their independence, some even to the point of murdering their enemies, husbands and lovers.

"Thank you, my dear Doctor," said Holmes. "Anything else, Constable?"

"Just one other thing, sir. I'm hoping you and the Inspector don't mind my bringing it to your attention."

"I am certain we shall appreciate your doing so. What is it?"

"It a letter we found, sir. There must have been a hundred letters, but this one, well, it rather stood out."

"And why was that?"

"It's from General Kitchener, sir, and addressed to Lord Vanderstone. It's dated four months ago, and it must have arrived here not long before he died."

"Right," said Lestrade. "Then don't stand there chatting about it. If you think it's important, read it to us."

"Yes, Inspector. Yes, sir. It's a bit of a delicate subject, and I wouldn't want what it says to get out to the Press, if you know what I mean."

"Fine. I know. Now read it."

The constable held the letter out in front of him. I could see the Kitchener coat of arms emblazoned on it. The constable cleared his throat and read.

"Like I said, it's addressed to Lord Vanderstone. And it starts off like this. 'Regarding your request received Monday last for a posthumous honor to be bestowed on your son, Captain Clayton of the Coldstream Guards.' Then it goes on, 'The loss of any young life in the service of King and Empire is always tragic, and I extend to you and your family my condolences and sympathy. However, with regret, I have no choice but to decline your request. I have received reliable reports that Captain Vanderstone had been engaging in actions unbecoming to an officer. Specifically, he had been involved in the acquiring and smuggling diamonds and gold from the Cape. In pursuit of these unlawful activities, he took his men into a district that other officers had warned him was highly dangerous. Directly as a result of his actions, he and all of his men, save one, were killed. Had he survived, he would now be facing a court-martial and the loss of his rank.' "

Constable Axline put the letter down in front of Lestrade. "I must say, not a pleasant letter for a father to get. I rather thought you might find it significant."

"It is, Constable," said Lestrade. "Very interesting indeed. Anything else to report?"

"Nothing that struck us as being particularly important, Inspector, sir. It's all laid out here in the room. Shall I have the trash taken away now? It's giving off a bit of a foul smell, as you may have noticed."

"Right. Please do that and——"

"If you would not mind," Holmes interrupted, "please leave it until I have had the opportunity to examine it. Allow me to suggest that we open the windows if the odor is objectionable."

"Right, Holmes. You can sort through the garbage," said Lestrade adding a roll of his eyes and a smirk. "But if you don't mind, I would like you to carry out the last interview first and sort the rubbish later. Have you made the Bayneses wait long enough?"

"I have. Please have them brought to the parlor."

Chapter Fourteen

The End of Slavery

"I do hope we have not interrupted your lunch, sir," said Holmes to Mr. Baynes as he was escorted into the parlor by a constable. Baynes did not deign to reply, and he and his wife sat down on the sofa and glared at us.

"I see no need," said Holmes, "to go over the events of last evening. We have taken your statements, and unless there is additional information you wish to share with us, I suggest we move on to other matters."

"There is no additional information," said Bentley Baynes. "So do get on with whatever questions you feel you have to ask and then get this nonsense over with. We are losing our patience with your unwelcome presence in our home "

"We shall be on our way as soon as our investigation has concluded," said Holmes with a not-particularly-sincere smile. "Now, sir, you just referred to this house as 'our home.' Is it *your home*? I had been led to understand that you lived in an entirely separate residence in Chelsea. Is that not correct?"

"We have a house there," said Baynes. "However, in keeping with the terms of Lord Vanderstone's will, we now are the owners, along with Mr. and Mrs. Vanderstone, of this house and of the estate property in St. Alban's."

"Are you now? Well, my best wishes on your good fortune. But do correct me if I am wrong. Is not the will relatively irrelevant? It leaves you with a handful of the lares and penates and not much more, does it not?"

"Kindly stop talking nonsense," said Baynes. "Cuthbert gave you a copy of the will, did he not? You can see that we were awarded a fair portion of the estate."

"And with the death of Lady Giselle, that portion has substantially increased, has it not?"

"It has, but our previous expectations were more than enough for us, and we were more than satisfied."

"Yes, yes. It is always good to be content with whatever good fortune befalls one," said Holmes. "But do tell, were you also satisfied with the shares you received in The Fidelity and Empire Trading and Investments Company Limited?"

"The *what*?"

"The firm into which almost all of the assets of your family were transferred."

"I don't know what you're talking—"

"Oh, Bentley," his wife interrupted, "of course we do."

"My dear, you—"

"No, Bentley, we are not going to mislead the police. Yes, gentlemen, we are fully aware of the secretive moving of all the family's properties and securities into that firm, and yes, we were not happy about it, not happy at all. And yes, we are much better off now that Giselle is dead. Is that what you want to know?"

"It is," said Holmes. "and did that attempt by Lady Giselle contribute to the animus felt against her?"

"Not at all," said Bentley Baynes, "families have to learn to get along. There were no hard feelings—"

"Bentley," said his wife, "you cannot say things like that. We all hated Giselle even before she pulled that stunt on us. Her doing so made us hate her all the more. So, yes, gentlemen, our reaction was what any sane person would have expected. We were furious with her."

"Well, yes, I suppose we were somewhat miffed," said her husband. "But what family in England does not have its squabbles? If that were grounds for murder, why every estate in the country would have someone being done away with."

"Speaking of your family's estate," said Holmes, "where did the money come from?"

"All money in England," said Bentley Baynes, "is printed by the Bank of England. Any other source—except for the American mint and other foreign currencies—would be counterfeit, and I assure you—"

"Bentley, stop being deliberately obtuse," said his wife. "Scotland Yard and Sherlock Holmes know what the Bank of England does. They want to know where my step-father and his father, dear old Grandpa Basil, made all their money. Is that not correct, gentlemen?"

"It is, madam," said Holmes. "What was the source of the family's wealth?"

"The slave trade."

"Madam? The slave trade ended in 1807. Slavery itself was abolished in the 1830s. That was several decades before Basil Vanderstone amassed his fortune."

"Oh please, Mr. Holmes, you really must brush up on your history. Slavery persisted in Cuba until 1886 and in Brazil until 1888. The Vanderstone clan made a fortune from it. Grandpa Basil and his Portuguese colleagues bought ships in New York and sailed them under the American flag so they could not be boarded by the British Navy. They kept on bringing slaves across from Angola and the Congo for years. When they could no longer do that without getting their ships impounded, they switched oceans and brought

Chinese and Indian coolies to America and all over the world. We would still be doing it today had not Giselle put a stop to it."

After hearing what Estelle Baynes said, Holmes, Lestrade and I were silent for a minute. I had not been aware of what she had just told us. Holmes, as he did often when confronted with data requiring absorption and reflection, lit a cigarette. He offered his case all around. Lestrade, Bentley Baynes, and I all declined. Mrs. Baynes accepted.

"From what you have said," said Holmes, "I assume that Lady Giselle had some moral qualms about the trafficking and exploitation of foreign workers."

Both Mr. and Mrs. Baynes broke into laughter.

"Clearly," said Bentley Baynes, "you did not know Giselle. She had not a moral bone in her body. She and Miss Holling extracted us from the coolie-supply business because they could see the writing on the wall. That trade is dying. It made much more economic sense to get out and invest in railways, and cotton and wool imports and all those other wonderful branches of commerce that pay healthy returns. And, by the way, her former partners were livid. They hated her every bit as much as we did. She played them for fools, swindled them. They didn't like that. They did not like that at all."

"Did they dislike her enough to murder her?" asked Holmes.

"Certainly. You can add them to a list of at least one hundred people we could name who would have gladly murdered her."

"Who then is at the top of your list? Please be frank. Whom do you say is the most likely suspect?

Mr. and Mrs. Baynes said nothing and sat and looked at each other for several moments.

"Go ahead, darling," said Mr. Baynes. "If I answer, you are just going to correct me."

"No, Bentley. You should tell them."

"Very well then, I would nominate one of those latter-day slavers. For the most part, they're Portuguese, and we all know what

75

they're like. Why don't you start making inquiries in the Docklands—"

"Good heavens, Bentley. Don't be absurd. Those swarthy sub-humans quite adored Giselle. They are making a fortune off of our old ships. In a year from now, when they realize they bought a pig in a poke, they'll be madder than hatters, but at the moment they all still think they were offered a bargain."

"Very well, my dear," replied Bentley Baynes with a sigh. "If not them, then who?"

"My vote goes to Doctor Quacksalver."

"Who?" said Holmes.

"That doctor of hers, the utter and complete quack. She was about to put him out of business, and the only way to stop her was to poison her. He was with her last evening and gave her the poisoned medicine. Obviously, Gladys saw what happened, and he had to get rid of her as well. That's what must have happened. I would bet five pounds on it."

"Would you indeed?" said Holmes. "Pray tell, how was it you knew she was poisoned? We had said nothing so far about the means of her death."

"Mr. Holmes, please. You have had six constables wandering around here all day, and the three youngest cannot hold on to such knowledge."

Lestrade harrumphed and looked around the room to see if any constables were present. Seeing none, he harrumphed again.

"Your point is taken, madam," said Holmes. "however, I see no reason for any animosity between lady Giselle and Dr. Anderson. When did they become enemies?"

"They weren't. One did not have to be an enemy of Giselle to have her stab you in the back. All one needed was to exist and appear to be successful and to have the misfortune of coming into contact with her. She reveled in the malicious joy of defeating people, trouncing them, seeing them brought down. To her, the thrill of power was utterly titillating."

"What then was she doing to him?"

"I believe, Mr. Holmes, it is generally referred to as blackmail."

"Over what? What had he done?"

"He was a complete fraud. She knew his credentials were phony, that his secret elixirs were nothing but snake oil. She threatened to have him exposed in the press and to ruin him if he did not pay her almost every farthing he collected. And why? Because she *could*."

"How do you know this?" asked Holmes.

"Because that miserable quack came to us and begged us to intervene on his behalf. We laughed and wished him good luck. He came here yesterday to grovel and beg one more time. She likely laughed in his face, and he had no choice but to get rid of her and, quite frankly, we are happy he did."

Once the Bayneses had gone, Holmes sat back and lit another cigarette. For several minutes he said nothing and puffed slowly.

"Inspector," he eventually said, "I believe we need to pay another visit to Dr. Anderson. Would you be able to leave here in about twenty minutes and accompany Dr. Watson and me back to Harley Street?"

Inspector Lestrade checked his watch. "It's time for me to go home for dinner. You go without me and let me know if you learn anything new."

Chapter Fifteen

Here, Drink This

D r. Garrett Anderson was not happy to see us.

"For pity's sake, what do you two want now?" was his welcome when we arrived at his surgery.

"Only a brief word," said Holmes. "You might be able to help us discover who was responsible for the death of Lady Giselle. I am sure you would not object to doing so, would you?"

He rolled his eyes and added a forced sigh of exasperation for good measure.

"Fine, then get on with it. What do you want?"

"I have been informed, sir, that Lady Giselle was demanding payments from you, is that correct?"

"Yes, and do you want to know what she demanded? Not that it matters much now that she is dead."

"If you do not mind, yes, I would like to know."

"Eighty percent of all income in excess of what is received in the current calendar year. And do you wish to see the contract signed between us in which the terms are stated in writing? After some vigorous discussions yesterday afternoon, we came to an amicable agreement."

I was surprised to hear him say that. Blackmail is not usually enshrined in a signed contract. From the look on Holmes's face, he was not expecting that either, but he immediately recovered and nodded.

"Yes, I would."

Anderson opened a drawer of his desk and extracted what appeared to be a sealed contract and thrust it in front of Holmes.

"Here. Read it. Or rather than waste more of my time while you do so, I will tell you its terms, and you can read it at your leisure. Take it home with you if you like. It is meaningless now."

"Pray, sir, what were the terms?"

"She was convinced that my elixirs had the potential for sales far beyond the bounds of London. If I would mix up vast barrels of them, bottle them, and paste on a label certifying that they were prepared in my laboratory and under my supervision, she would undertake to advertise them throughout Europe and America, and eventually Asia and South America. She would arrange distributors and fulfill the orders. She predicted my sales would increase twenty, fifty or even a hundredfold."

"And you agreed to that?"

"I would be a fool not to. My current sales within London were excluded. She took on all the risk and would do most of the work, Or, more likely, would find coolies to do it for her. Except for the cost of mixing up a brew now and then, which would not be done until orders were received, I risked nothing. If you or Dr. Watson make me the same offer, I would sign it. Mind you, I doubt you have anywhere near the business mind of Giselle."

"No doubt you are right on that one. However, what would stop you from stealing her idea, doing the advertising and fulfillment yourself, killing her and keeping one hundred percent of the income?"

Anderson looked offended for a minute and then relaxed into a mocking laugh.

"Because, my dear Mr. Detective, I could not be bothered. In case you had not noticed, I already have a splendid existence. Taking on all the extra work such a venture would require is not my cup of tea. I guess I am just too content and lazy."

"Why would you agree to allowing her to take such an unfair cut of the income. Why not argue for fifty-fifty?"

"Oh, I did. Believe me, I did. I started at demanding a third. She started at ninety percent. We settled at eighty. Giselle is, or I should say *was,* a very determined negotiator."

"Did she threaten you in any way if you did not agree? Did she threaten to expose you as a fraud and ruin you?"

"Ah, you clearly did not know her well at all, did you? Lady Giselle Vanderstone never threatened. She merely *explained.*"

Holmes paused for a moment and took a different tack.

"Regardless, sir, there have been suspicions voiced that you inserted a poison into her elixir and that she died from ingesting it."

"Voiced, no doubt, by the members of her family. They hated her, in case you had not noticed that either. I had nothing to gain by doing such a deed and rather an easy new line of income to lose."

"Then you would not mind proving so by taking a swallow of your elixir yourself."

Holmes pulled out from his pocket the small bottle of yellow fluid we had found in Lady Giselle's handbag and thrust it in front of Anderson. Inwardly, I smiled and wondered what excuse the charlatan doctor would come up with for not imbibing. To my utter shock and horror, he accepted the bottle, slowly and deliberately removed the stopped, smirked at Holmes, raised it to his mouth and took not one but two large gulps.

"Will that do, Mr. Holmes?" he said. "Now, if you have no more games to play, kindly leave my premises and get on with your amateur pursuits of criminals."

Holmes smirked back at him and turned to me. "Come, Watson, we have work to do."

As soon as we were out on the pavement, I grabbed him by the arm.

"Holmes, that man will be dead in minutes. You murdered him. Have you gone mad?"

"No, my friend, I fear I have not. Immediately before coming here, I spent a few minutes in the kitchen and emptied the bottle into another container, thoroughly steamed and rinsed it and refilled it with a similar concoction, minus the cyanide."

We hailed a cab and asked the driver to take us back to Primrose Hill

"Very well then," I said, "I suppose you can eliminate Dr. Anderson off your list of possible suspects."

He did not respond and instead took out a cigarette and puffed slowly until we had reached Marylebone Road. Then he brought his fist down on his thigh and muttered an oath.

"No. I cannot. That man may be an arrogant fraudster, but he is not stupid. He knew I would never offer him poison and run the risk of killing him. He knew what I was handing him had to be safe. Did you see the smirk on his face when he took it from me?"

"I did, but that could have meant anything. I suspect he smirks several times a day. I confess to knowing proper doctors who do so as well."

"Perhaps you're right. But for now, I cannot altogether cease to suspect him. Though. perhaps I can move him down the list."

"So, back to the hated and hating family?"

"Precisely."

Chapter Sixteen

The Play's the Thing

A few blocks further on, we turned north on Baker Street on our way back up to Primrose Hill. I had been thinking as we traveled and posed a question to Holmes.

"What did you think about those slavers and steamship owners who moved human cargo? Any chance they might have been upset enough with Lady Giselle to want her dead?"

"They are certainly an unsavory lot, but I have no reason to doubt what we were told by Mrs. Baynes to the effect that they are still making good coin from the business Lady Giselle sold them."

"Umm ... Holmes ... did you just say you have no reason to doubt something you were told by Mrs. Baynes?"

He laughed. "A point well-taken, Watson. I truly have no idea yet what of her words to believe and what not."

"But you don't think we should make some inquiries down in the docklands?"

"They are not at the top of my list at the moment. They may have had reason to want to be rid of her, but there was no mention of a visit by any one of them last evening. It is highly unlikely one of them could have snuck into the house, made his way to her room, poisoned the elixir and then escaped utterly unheard and unseen. These things happen in sensationalist theater productions, but the committing of crimes is much more mundane."

"I suppose so," I said but was not entirely sure. *What if,* I thought, *one of the family members was in league with the smugglers?* Holmes, however, was still fixated on the family.

"Watson," he said, as we pulled into the driveway of the Vanderstone house, "given that you have been thinking about this crime—for that I give you credit—pray tell, who amongst the family members do you consider the most likely to be the killer? They all had reason and the opportunity to do so, but one of them went ahead and took the action. Whom do you suspect?"

"If I had to name anyone, I would have to settle on the cousin, that Cuthbert Molesworth fellow."

"An interesting choice. Your fellow writer. Why him? He seemed somewhat adoring of you."

"Flattery is the food of fools," I said, quoting Mr. Swift. "I have always been leery of the obsequious, fawning type. Granted, I am now a somewhat successful author, and he is just starting his career, but I never had to kiss the boots of anyone else. I earned my stripes. Good writers welcome hard critiques, not fulsome praise. Master Cuthbert was a bit too much, if you know what I mean."

"I do. Another point well-made and well-taken."

A constable I had not met before was standing guard at the door.

"A change of the guard?" I asked as we entered the house.

"Yes, sir. Inspector Lestrade wanted to make sure that as many as possible had a chance at this posting. Quite the fascinating assignment, it is. A murder case—now two murders—and getting to watch Sherlock Holmes at work. Right fine way to spend a summer weekend."

"And how are our inmates doing? Anything untoward to report?"

"No, sir. They are all getting along rather well. In truth, a bit too well if you ask me. They're a pretty jolly lot for ones who just had a member of the family and a maid murdered. They're busying themselves with cards and charades in the dining room and doing a lot of giggling and laughing."

"Makes you wonder, Constable, what they were up to?" I said.

"Must say, sir, it does do a bit of that."

"And I must say, it does me too. All right then, just keep up the good work, and maybe Sherlock Holmes will solve the case in front of your very eyes. What would you say to that?"

"It would give me a fine story to tell for years to come, sir."

"Enough chit-chat," said Holmes as he proceeded to the library. I followed him.

As we were passing the dining room, one of the women called out to us.

"Yoo-hoo! Mr. Detective! Dr. Watson! You really must come and join us. We're having such a good time."

It was Mrs. Constance Vanderstone shouting to us, and her speech was somewhat slurred, thanks, no doubt, to the empty bottles of gin on the sideboard. She would not let up.

"Come on, now, Mr. Holmes. See if you can solve a mystery. Or are you afraid to try?"

She babbled on about their game of *pantomime charades,* which, having been imported from France, had become quite the rage in the homes of the idle rich. I sighed and ignored her, but Holmes grabbed my forearm.

"We shall join them for a round," he said.

"Have you lost your senses?" I whispered back to him. "They are all drunk, stupid and obnoxious."

"Occasionally the most banal behavior can be revealing. We can depart immediately if it proves a complete waste of time."

The five assembled members of the family let out a cheer and applause as we assumed our places at the dining room table.

"Welcome, welcome," enthused Mrs. Vanderstone. "Let me esplain how thish works."

She went on to state that the next round would require the participants to guess the name of a play by Shakespeare based solely on the silent actions of the player. Whoever guessed first won a point.

"It sounds positively intriguing," said Holmes, "but allow us to observe a few rounds before we join in the game."

The first up was Bentley Baynes. He moved to the head of the table and took a bow. Then he held up one finger.

"One word!" shouted the four other players in unison, whereupon they all laughed and gave themselves a round of applause.

It had been many years since I was forced to study the works of the Bard, but I vaguely remembered that almost all of the plays that were popularly known by a one-word title had, in fact, several words in the official name. The full and proper name of *Othello* was *The Tragedy of Othello, Moor of Venice.* That was seven words, so that one was out. Wracking my brain, I landed on *Coriolanus* as the only one of the thirty-nine with a one-word title. I was tempted to shout it out before Baynes got any farther but, abiding by Holmes's agreement, I had to content my soul with sitting back and feeling more than somewhat smug.

Bentley Baynes then sprang into action. In a succession of quick moves, he put his hands on each side of his head and pretended to lift it off his shoulders. Then he transferred the head to one hand, held it out in front of him and affected a look of sadness. Cuthbert Molesworth responded immediately.

"Ohh! I've got it! *Alas, poor Yorick, I knew him well.* Hamlet!!" His outburst was followed by a round of applause. I knew then that I was not surrounded by Shakespearian scholars. Not only was the play's proper name *The Tragedy of Hamlet, Prince of Denmark,* but that was not what Hamlet said after being given Yorick's skull. What he said was, *Alas, poor Yorick. I knew him, Horatio."* Literary accuracy was clearly not included in the rules of the game, and we were on to the next round. Having won the first, Cuthbert Molesworth took his place at the head of the table.

He closed his eyes as if to let us know that he was concentrating intently, trying to decide on which play to perform. He then smiled and nodded and, holding his hands out in front of himself, he pretended to grasp a vertical object and, with a strenuous effort, pull it out of the ground. Then he walked awkwardly, holding the object in front of his body.

Nobody said a word. He gestured for us all to ignore his first attempt and then, with eyes half-closed, he gazed up at the ceiling and staggered for a few steps until he was standing directly behind Sherlock Holmes. Then he reached his hand out, grasped an object and pulled it down. In a dramatic gesture, he held the object in his right hand and with it made a stabbing motion into Holmes's back. Both of the women shouted at once.

"Macbeth!! You're Lady Macbeth!"

Not wanting to be left out, Jefferson Vanderstone started quoting, "*Is this a dagger which I see before me, The handle toward my hand? Come, let me clutch thee. I have thee not, and yet I see thee still.*" He might have carried on had his wife not interrupted him.

"Enough, my dear," she said and, assuming herself to have won the round, took her place at the head of the table while the others gave Molesworth his applause.

Constance Vanderstone held up three fingers, indicating a three-word title. This was followed by one finger, to tell us she would act out the first word, and then she laid three fingers on her forearm, letting us know there were three syllables. Then one finger came down, indicating the first syllable. To convey that syllable, she pretended to grasp a set of oars in her hands and pulled her hands back into her body.

"Scull? You're in a single sculls?" said Bentley Baynes.

"No, my dear," said his wife. "She's *rowing*. It's ROW, like *Row-me-o*, as in *Romeo and Juliet!*"

"Oh, yes, of course. Well done darling," said Bentley Baynes, giving his wife a gentle pat on the top of her head.

I felt a kick to my ankle from Holmes. He was getting up and gestured to me to follow.

"Thank you," he said to the family, "for the amusing game. Unfortunately, we have to get back to work."

"Oh no, Mr. Holmes, must you?" said Estelle Baynes. "It will not be nearly as much fun without you."

He ignored her, and we walked out of the room. As we were departing, a roar of laughter went up, and I guessed that one of them had made some ignorant or vulgar facial expression that the others found uproarious.

"You were right, Watson," Holmes said as we entered the library. "It was a complete waste of time."

"What, in heaven's name, were you hoping to see?"

"I suspect that all of them know which one of them poisoned Lady Giselle's medicine. I was observing them closely to see if there were any signs of deference, any indication of newly acquired status amongst them as a result."

"And was there?"

"No. They are all equally deplorable. Come, now, back to work."

As with the other rooms on the house, the library was adorned with paintings and artifacts from Africa. The foot of an elephant served as a wastebasket, stuffed heads of antelope and gazelle were mounted on the walls above the bookshelves, and crossed spears and decorated shields filled any spaces on the walls that were not occupied with books. In several strategic locations, however, there were photographs of what I assumed had been Lord Vanderstone and his first wife and a toddler who was, no doubt, the now-deceased Captain Clayton Vanderstone. The first Lady Vanderstone was strikingly blond, as was her young son. Later photographs, several of them, must have been taken after the death of the mother and were of His Lordship and his two offspring at various stages in their growing up. At one time, I concluded, they must have been a happy family. Curiously, there were no photographs of the second Lady Vanderstone nor of Lord Vanderstone's step-children.

The tables in the room were laid out as they had been earlier in the day, with orderly piles of papers, toiletries, articles of clothing, personal effects and assorted piles of rubbish. The food scraps had been removed, for which I was thankful.

"I shall need at least an hour to conduct a thorough review of all this," said Holmes. "Can you stave off your need for dinner until then, my dear Doctor?"

"I'm sure I can manage," I said. "How can I help you here?"

"You can't. You would only be in my way."

"Then why did you not say something as we came up Baker Street? I could have gotten out rather than coming here and wasting my time."

"Because I need you for another task, one for which you are far better suited than I am."

"All right, and what might that be?"

"I need you to fetch a bottle of rum from the liquor cabinet and go and have a soldier-to-soldier chat with the groom."

Chapter Seventeen

Swapping War Stories

"I can certainly do that," I said, "but what in the world for?"

"After you have softened him up with rum and old war stories, you need to interrogate him about the lucrative fraud Lord Vanderstone was carrying on when charging stud fees for that horse I was riding."

"Holmes, that horse won the Grand National. There's no fraud in that. Stud fees for thoroughbreds like him are always dear."

"Correct, they are, but also incorrect. The horse on which I was riding was not Starless Midnight. He was a decent horse who had been fraudulently disguised to appear like the steeplechase winner. When I took my tumble, I soiled my hands with grass stains and dirt and such. However, as I wiped them off, I also noticed that I was wiping off some blotches of black dye. Whilst leading the spirited beast back to the stables, I looked at the spot on his crest and noticed traces of white. As I walked him back to the stables, I spotted a few more traces of white on his back fetlocks. I suspect that he has *stars* in several places on his body. Those spots were dyed black, and he has been pretending."

"Then what happened to the real winner?"

"I have no idea. All I know is that the horse on which I was riding was indeed a fine animal, but it was not Starless Midnight. Lord Vanderstone had been operating a fraudulent stud service business for the past four years at least. I would not be surprised if he was raking in several hundred pounds a week."

"Then should you be looking at any members of the horse racing lot as well? Maybe one of them found out Vanderstone had been cheating them. Money like that is enough to lead someone to kill, wouldn't you say?"

"True enough, Watson. It is, of course, far less likely than a million and a half pounds as a motive for murder. But it is still sufficient to encourage someone to kill, especially if compounded with anger and revenge. Therefore, I shall continue to concentrate my investigations on the family and request that you learn all you can about the phony horse."

I raided the liquor cabinet in the library and found a half-full bottle of excellent dark rum, a brand that I remembered as having been shared by my fellow soldiers in the Afghan Wars many years earlier. I slipped it under my suit jacket and made my way out the back of the house to the stables.

The stables had been freshly whitewashed and were neat as a pin. The bridles and tack were hung and shelved in a uniform pattern, and the floors had been swept clean. There were six stalls, four of which were occupied by fine-looking animals. Not one became the least bit jumpy as I walked past them, and all the coats were gleaming from care and constant brushing.

Othniel Clarke, the groom, had a room at the far end of the stables, and I gave a firm knock on his wide-open door.

"Good afternoon, soldier!" I said, but there was no response. So, I uttered it again, this time shouting.

From somewhere not too far away, a voice shouted back.

"Be there in a minute. Take yourself in and sit down."

The room was spartan and spotless. The bed was not only made but the blankets were drawn tight, and the corners tucked in at perfect angles. The few clothes on hangers were all uniformly arranged and spaced. That was not surprising for a man who had recently returned from military service where *a place for everything and everything in its place* is considered equal to holy writ. What struck me as odd, however, was the collection of books. A copy of Mahan's *The Influence of Sea Power Upon History* was lying on the bedside table. Underneath it was the *History of the Peloponnesian War.* In a small bookcase, I observed the classic texts by Homer, Virgil, Vitruvius, Plato, Aristotle, Plato and even a well-worn edition of Ovid.

This young soldier was clearly intent on bettering himself, and I felt somewhat proud of him for doing so.

"Good afternoon, Dr. Watson," Othniel Clarke chimed as he entered. He clicked his heels together and saluted me in a somewhat exaggerated manner. "How can I help you? Fancy going for another ride before supper?"

"Not at all, Private Clarke," I said. "My friend, Sherlock Holmes, is occupied inside the house for the next hour or so, and I thought I might enjoy a chat with a fellow soldier, helped along, of course, by a friendly libation or two."

As I spoke, I put the bottle of rum on the small coffee table with a decided thud.

"Aww, Doctor, that was very kind of you. Sorry to be such a poor host, but I do not even have glasses to drink from. Would you mind using a teacup?"

"It cannot hurt the taste, so why not."

I started the conversation by commenting on his impressive collection of books. He shrugged.

"I'm trying to improve myself. I don't want to still be a groom when I'm fifty. Fighting for my country didn't do me any good, so I thought if I learned enough, I might get accepted as a school teacher in some small village where they have a hard time finding teachers. Nobody complains about a teacher who is over fifty and has a scarred face as long as he's willing to live in some god-forsaken corner of nowhere and teach the local children."

I agreed and tried to pass along a few words of encouragement. Then, as always happens when soldiers get together, we started on our stories.

All soldiers have memories. Some can never be told. They bring back scenes in our minds we need to forget. But all soldiers also have a few tales to tell, stories about the pranks played on sergeants, the jokes, about sneaking out at night to visit the bar in the village and crawling back into camp before dawn, and stories about seeing strange, wondrous corners of the world and being lost in awe. For nearly an hour, Othniel Clarke and I swapped such stories, gradually embellishing them in direct proportion to the rum consumed.

By the time his second teacup had been drained, and I was still on my first, I felt the time had come to shift the conversation, and I asked him about the war itself. For the next few minutes, he gave his opinion of the tactics that were followed by the British.

"Until we finally broke the siege at Ladysmith, we were incompetent. Then they tried using the creeping barrage and that worked. But then the Boers switched to guerilla tactics and started hitting us from every direction. We would not have won if Kitchener hadn't rounded up their women and children into his camps and scorched their farms."

He carried on—the rum was talking now—and gave his opinion of many of the battles and skirmishes and of what our incompetent generals should have done. I let him go on and kept re-filling his cup.

"You know, it wouldn't hurt," I said, "for you to talk about what happened to you. It might be a good thing."

"What do you want to know?"

"About what happened when you were almost killed."

"We thought we were safe, and we were ambushed. That's all."

"Shouldn't your captain have known better than to make camp where you did?"

"Some experts sitting in armchairs on Pall Mall said he should have. But they weren't there. Our captain did what he thought was best, and we followed him. We trusted him. And now he's dead, so I'm not going to say aught against him."

It occurred to me that he likely never heard of the allegations brought against his captain, and I decided I was not going to be the one who broke the news. Instead, I brought the conversation back to the present and the stables.

"How long," I asked, "had Lord Vanderstone been using another horse as a stand-in for Starless Midnight and taking fees for fraudulent stud services?"

Over the years, I have noticed that imbibing in alcohol has a variety of effects on men. Some become nasty and pugnacious, ceasing entirely to act like gentlemen. Others become excessively joyful, giggling and guffawing at anything that passes for humor. Others yet withdraw, acting sullen and taciturn. And finally, there are those, like Mr. Othniel Clarke, who lose their inhibitions and are congenially loquacious and talkative.

Othniel became utterly chatty.

"Hey there, doc. Who told you that? You want to know about that ruse? You want me to tell you all about it?"

"I do indeed."

"Well, it all happened before I arrived, but Lady Vanderstone, bless her heart, told me all about it. You see, it was like this. It all happened up on the family estate in St. Albans. A month after he won the Grand National, the real Starless Midnight got taken out for a hard run, and his rider pushed him way too hard. The poor beast up and had his heart burst and flopped over and died. Real sad it was. There was already a score or more mares in line to have him do what stallions do to mares, if you know what I mean."

"I do. Go on."

"His Honorable Lordship was charging three hundred pounds a tail-tickling, and he wasn't about to give that up. No, like Antony said of Brutus, he was an honorable man. He'd already taken the money from the mares' owners, and being a reliable man of commerce, he wasn't about to welch on his agreement. So, what does he do? He and the previous groom—the one I replaced—they come up with the idea of taking another one of their stallions—real name was *Feet of Silver*—and they got themselves some hair dye like some ladies use when they start to go grey, and they took a couple of toothbrushes and fixed up that stallion right proper. Now, he was a right good horse, he was, but he weren't no champion. Well, there's no guarantee in the stud business that whatever pops out of the mare is going to be a champion, but there's always a chance. And that's what makes horse races, as they say."

"It is indeed. Is it still going on?"

"No, Her Ladyship, God rest her sweet soul, put a stop to it."

"Quite the one for being honest and upright in business, was she?" I asked.

He laughed. "Ah, sorry there, Doc. I adored her for what she did for me, but she weren't no saint. What she was, was smart as they come. Aye, she was that and more. She could see that all it would take is for one of the owners to notice silver feet on his foal, and he'd start asking questions. If'n the truth were to leak out, and the truth will out, as they say, it would be a big scandal and all over the press, and that would be bad for business. So, the painting of the stallion had to end, and so it did."

"So, do tell, did anyone of the owners who was swindled ever catch on? Were any threats ever made?"

"Her Ladyship said that no one yet had caught on. So, you can believe what you want, Doc."

"And you clearly believed her."

Again, he laughed. "Aw, Doc, don't go asking me that. Like I said, I adored her, worshipped the ground she walked on, but *truth*? Naw. Bless her heart, she could look you straight in the eye and tell you that two and two was five and say it with a straight face, and you would believe her. And the next day, she could tell you it was three, and you would still believe her. Truth? Truth was whatever served her purpose at the time. I shouldn't be saying this—*de mortuis nil nisi bonum* and all that—but the rest of the family, they called her Lady Macbeth or Jezebel and names like that, and I have to give it to them, they did have their reasons."

By now, he had finished his third teacup and had started to slur his speech, and I knew that any further interrogation would be useless. So, we went back to swapping a few more war stories and laughing.

When an hour had passed, I stood up and walked back, not entirely steadily, to find Holmes. He was winding up his examination of the materials in the library, and I offered him a shot of fine rum. He declined, as was his wont. That was fortunate, as I subsequently noticed that the bottle was empty.

"All right," I said, perhaps more loudly than was necessary, "I'd say it's time to go home for supper. It's almost seven and I'm hungry. How about you?"

He said nothing, but he pulled his personal effects together and walked out of the house. I followed him out to Avenue Road, and then we walked back to Baker Street. All the way home, he said nothing.

Mrs. Hudson had left us a fine cold supper, which I consumed heartily and which Holmes picked at in a desultory manner. Other than asking me to pass the salt and thanking me for refilling his cup of tea, he said nothing.

As soon as the dishes were cleared, he became animated and demanded that I repeat word for word the conversation between myself and Othniel Clarke. I did so, and he nodded, asked more questions, and took notes.

"Do you suppose," I asked, "that the fraud was serious enough for someone to take revenge by killing Lord Vanderstone?"

"The crowd who raise and race horses are a passionate and irrational lot," he said. "Otherwise, they would not wager a farthing on a horse race. It would not be the first time that one of their coterie killed another over some altercation connected to a horse. That the stud fraud was connected remains a possibility but not a strong one, and there is no immediate connection to the murder of Lady Giselle Vanderstone several months later. Let me think about it."

Throughout the remainder of the evening, I read, and Holmes alternated between pacing back and forth and sitting in his armchair with his long legs drawn up under his body and his eyes closed.

"Care to tell me what you are thinking?" I asked as the hour was approaching ten.

"Ask me in the morning."

Chapter Eighteen

Pick a Card

 **"W**ATSON, WAKE UP!"

I felt the friendly but firm hand of Sherlock Holmes on my shoulder, shaking me awake.

"Wha ... what time is it?" I muttered.

"It's five o'clock. We have to get back to the Vanderstone house. Please, my friend, make haste."

"What now?"

"Never mind. I'll shall explain on route. Please hurry."

I washed and dressed as quickly as I could. Holmes was waiting for me at the top of the stairs and started down as soon as I appeared in the front room. I caught up to him on the pavement of Baker Street. He was moving at a forced march, with his arms swinging slightly and fists clenched.

"Merciful heavens," I said whilst catching my breath, "what is it?"

"I do not take kindly to being mocked. Certainly not by those abhorrent miscreants."

"Mocked you? How? They don't want you around, and they made that clear, but when did they mock you?"

"During their silly game."

"Oh, come now, Holmes. That was Shakespeare. Surely you don't think he had you in mind when he wrote the plays."

"Watson, instead of making inane remarks, please think. In *Hamlet,* how does the Queen die?"

I knew that one. "The king, Claudius, puts a poisoned pearl in the wine goblet, and she drank from it in a toast to Hamlet."

"And in the play within the play, how does the king die?"

"Well, yes, *the play's the thing,* right? Poison is poured into his ear while he's sleeping."

"Correct. And Romeo. How does he die?"

"He stabs himself."

"No, Watson, that was Juliet. Romeo drinks the vial of poison he bought from the apothecary. Can you not see what they were doing? They were making a joke out of poisoning Giselle. They were laughing about it and laughing at me whilst they were at it."

"Oh, I see. But what about Lady Macbeth?"

"That is one of the names they called Giselle. They had her stab me, and they thought it a great joke. But I am about to turn the tables on them. By noon, I shall have the entire revolting lot of them all under arrest and on their way to the gallows."

"How?"

"Don't talk. Just observe."

We kept walking quickly up Avenue Road toward Primrose Hill. Holmes was not interested in chatting, but I still had one question.

"What about when Molesworth pretended to pull a pole out of the ground and stagger forward with it."

"Please, Watson, it wasn't a pole, it was a tree, and he was carrying it toward Dunsinane."

"Oh, so Birnam Wood and all that."

"Yes, now please, let me think."

The time had only just past half-five, and the streets were empty in the cool of the early morning. A constable was still standing guard at the Vanderstone's London house and was surprised to see us arriving before anyone in the household was awake.

"Good morning, Constable," said Holmes as we entered. "All is well? Nothing untoward last evening?"

"Nothing one could call criminal, Mr. Holmes, if you know what I mean. They just had dinner and sat around and played games and laughed and drank until ten, when they all went to bed. Quite the jolly lot. Seemed as pleased as punch with themselves, they did."

"As I might have expected," said Holmes.

I followed him into the library. Another constable stood guard over the room and assured us that nothing had been disturbed or even touched since we had departed the premises late the previous day.

"Excellent," said Holmes, with that look on his face that I have come to know over the years. He quietly settled himself into place at one of the tables, his eyes gleaming like a lion about to pounce on its prey.

"Tell me, Watson, if you were hosting a dinner for five close members of your family who all lived in London and knew each other quite well, would you need name cards at the dining table?"

"I couldn't say. I don't have any close family in London."

"Yes, of course. Then try to use such imagination as you have and pretend you do. Would you need name cards?"

"For five people? No. For a dozen or more, yes, but not for that few."

"I agree. Yet in front of me are the name cards that our fine constable retrieved from the trash. Does that not strike you are curious?"

"Not really. Every family has its own way of doing things."

"Yes, and at five o'clock this morning, it struck me that this family had a way that was odd, even for them."

He took out his glass and carefully examined each of the cards, and then he held them up to his nose and sniffed. A smile of triumphant satisfaction spread across his face.

"Until now, I have been attempting to discern which member of the family infused Giselle's bottle of elixir with cyanide. However, it was not an individual member."

"Then who was it?"

"It was all of them. They clearly came to some agreement that they had to get rid of Giselle, and they acted in concert. If you closely observe the back of each of these cards and smell it, you will see the tiny flecks of cyanide powder on each of them. They all bear the faint odor of almonds. Each of them placed a small amount of powder onto the back of the folded card and tapped it into the elixir bottle. I suspect that they divided the tasks amongst themselves so that every one of them had a hand in it. One of them must have slipped into Lady Giselle's room after she had gone to sleep—"

"But surely she might have heard them."

"Do recall that she told us she was very weary when she went up to her room. I suspect that they adulterated her food with laudanum to help send her into a sound sleep. Once they had all put their share of poison into the bottle and given it a good shake, someone else likely replaced it on her bedside table. They all took part in the murder. What they did not suspect was that she would wake up, overhear their gloating and come on her bicycle to see me."

"What about the maid?"

"Ah, she must have seen what was happening and confronted one of them, who then suffocated her."

"And the doctor? He lied to you about not having any other members of the family as his patients."

"Yes, but I am convinced that he did not lie about being too lazy to bother expanding his business and happy to do little or nothing and still take twenty percent of significant worldwide sales from the expanded advertising and distribution organized by Lady Giselle."

"Well, as you say, when you have eliminated—"

"Precisely."

"What happens now?"

"I'll have one of the constables place a call to Inspector Lestrade and ask that he come here straight away. I will explain my conclusions to him, and then we confront the gang of murderers."

Lestrade confirmed that he would arrive by eight o'clock. Whilst waiting for him, I wrote my notes on this case, and Holmes took himself for a celebratory stroll through the park, accompanied by his beloved pipe.

As I was sitting in the library, Bentley Baynes appeared in the doorway, clad in his dressing gown and, I assumed, on his way to the breakfast table.

"Scribble, scribble, scribble, eh, Dr. Watson? Another thin silly book? I'm sure your mother will buy a copy." He laughed and walked on. I confess I may have gloated inwardly thinking about the unpleasant surprise he was going to be handed in the near future.

Chapter Nineteen

The Groom Speaks

Inspector Lestrade and three more constables arrived at ten minutes to eight and joined Holmes and me in the library. Holmes closed the door so that family members could not eavesdrop, and then he methodically and thoroughly led Lestrade through the evidence and his conclusions.

When he had finished, Lestrade leaned back in his chair and folded his arms across his chest. "Right, clever as always, Mr. Holmes. I'm convinced that what you say happened is indeed what happened. But there's not enough there to stand up in court. Who's to say that these five were the ones that put the cyanide on the name cards and tapped it into what's-her-name's elixir bottle? They can all just deny it was them, and there's no proof. How about a witness or two?"

"I suspect that the now-deceased maid saw what was happening and paid for it with her life."

"A lot of good that does, Holmes. What about the groom?"

"Extremely unlikely that he was present and witnessed anything."

"But we did catch him eavesdropping on the first meeting with the family, didn't we? I'll wager he was listening in on the plan for murder. I'll have one of my constables go and fetch him."

Five minutes later, Constable Axline appeared in the library with Othniel Clarke in tow. The young soldier looked terribly ill-at-ease and looked at me, his countenance pleading.

"At ease, Private Clarke," I said. "Nothing to worry about. Just some routine questions."

"Oh, thank you, Doctor. It was a bit of a shock, it was, when a policeman comes and orders you away from your work. Didn't know what to think."

"What you need to think," said Lestrade, "is to remember what happened on Friday evening. Where were you?"

"Here, sir, at the house and mostly in my room out back in the stables, that is after offering to any of them to go riding, but they didn't want to, and so I put all the tack away and went to my room, and I didn't go out to the pub or anything like that, if that's what you're asking me, sir."

"I'm not asking you that. You've already proved you like to eavesdrop, so I'm asking you if you were eavesdropping on the five family members after Lady Giselle departed from the dining room for the evening? Well, were you?"

"I ... I might have overheard a word or two, sir. Just by accident as I was walking by, maybe, sir."

"Young man! It is a criminal offense to lie to the police. Now tell the truth, were you eavesdropping on them?"

The poor chap's disfigured face blushed deeply, glowing red in blotches and streaks where the skin had not been scarred. I felt compelled to say something.

"Relax, soldier. It would be a very good thing if you were eavesdropping and can remember what you heard. You would be an excellent help to Inspector Lestrade. Now, just let us know what you heard."

"And do be precise and concise," added Holmes. "But do not omit any significant details. Your report, Mr. Clarke."

With his eyes firmly fixed on his shoes, the young soldier gave a remarkably coherent account of what he had overheard on Friday evening.

"Where were you whilst you were hearing all this?" asked Lestrade.

"Standing right behind the dining-room door, sir. I could hear everything and see some through the crack against the hinges."

"You saw them as well?"

"Yes, Inspector, sir. But not everything. Only what I could see through the crack."

"Fine. Go on."

"Well, like I said already, sir, they had been having quite a few drinks after dinner, at least they sounded like a bunch of rich toffs who were drunk, and then the cousin, Mr. Molesworth, he announces that he has a new game for everybody. He calls it *How to Murder Lady Macbeth.* And they all laugh and cheer. And then he explains it. He pulls out of his pocket a large test tube, and he says it's full of cyanide—"

"Did you see him do that?" asked Lestrade.

"No, sir, but he must have had something because Mrs. Baynes, she says, 'Let me see that test tube," and so does Mr. Vanderstone. I couldn't see them saying that, but I know their voices, so I know who said it. And then he explains how they are all going to cooperate and get rid of Lady Giselle. And he says, 'Bring the name tags I put in front of you and follow me. And then they all went upstairs, real quiet like they did, to the door of Lady Giselle's rooms."

"Did you see what they did up there?" asked Lestrade.

"No, sir. Sorry, sir. I couldn't see them without them seeing me. But I could hear them a bit. They were whispering, but I heard Mrs. Vanderstone say she would go into Lady Giselle's room, and then everyone was quiet until she came back and then Mr. Molesworth tells them all to hold out their cards and then it got all quiet and then

Mrs. Baynes, she says she will go back into the room and then she comes back out, and they all come back down to the parlor and have a big laugh. And then they laughed about getting rid of Lady Giselle and saying that she would be dead in the morning, and that was all I heard."

"And what did you do then," said Lestrade.

"I waited for quite a bit until they all went to bed so they wouldn't see me. Then I snuck up to Lady Giselle's rooms and to wake her up and tell her that they were all trying to kill her. But she wasn't there. She must've known what they were up to, and I guess she overheard them talking because soon after that, around midnight, she comes out to the stables and asks me to fetch her bicycle and she says she's going off to talk to Mr. Sherlock Holmes and that's the last I saw her, and that's the truth, sir."

"It bloody well better be," said Lestrade. "But yesterday morning, you lied to us. You said the last time you had seen her was before supper when she went for a walk with her doctor. Why did you not tell us all this when we spoke to you before?"

Yet again, Othniel Clarke blushed and started to stammer. "I'm … I'm sorry sir. I was afraid that I told you I was the last one to see her alive that you would think I killed her. I'd be tried for murder, and the jury would take one look at my ugly face and decide I must be a killer."

He turned to me with a pathetic look on his scarred face. "I'm sorry, Doctor. Please don't let them send me to prison. I tried to help, honest I did."

"All right, then," said Lestrade. "That's all we need from you. You can go back to your room."

"Before you go," said Holmes, "there is something I need to clarify. By what name did Lady Giselle address you or call for you?"

"Usually she'd call me Private Clarke, seeing as that was what I was when I served under her brother, Captain Vanderstone. Sometimes she'd call me *brother's boy* or maybe *brother's private* or something along those lines, sir. Will that be all, sir?"

"That's all," said Holmes. "You may go back to your chores, but do not leave the grounds."

As soon as he was out of the room and the door closed behind him, Holmes asked Lestrade, "A reasonably decent witness, Inspector?"

"To conspiracy to commit murder, maybe. To murder itself, not nearly good enough. But we can fix that."

"Mind if I ask you how?"

"By good old-fashioned police tactics, Holmes. We turn them against each other."

Chapter Twenty

Talk to My Lawyer

Friendly chatter was emanating from the dining room as we entered. It ceased as soon as the five breakfasters saw us. Lestrade bade them a cheerful *Good morning,* and the three of us sat down on the side of the table that was not occupied.

Bentley Baynes let out a sigh. In a voice and manner that was somewhere between truculent and snide, he uttered several words I have chosen not to record and let us know that we were not welcome.

"Fret not, sir," said Lestrade, affecting a tone of conciliation. "We will not be here for long, but then again, neither will any of you." He pasted a forced grin on his face.

"And just what do you mean by that?" demanded Baynes.

"What I mean is that I am about to tell you what took place here on Friday evening, and then all of us will be on our way out of here. So, listen carefully."

Five pairs of eyes were trained on the inspector. Even I detected traces of apprehension behind them as Lestrade held forth.

"We have acquired evidence indicating that all five of you conspired to murder Lady Giselle Vanderstone by adulterating her bottle of medicine with cyanide. You, Mr. Cuthbert, acquired the poison and each of you held out your folded name cards as he tapped a small amount of cyanide into them. Mrs. Vanderstone entered Lady Giselle's bedroom whilst she was sleeping and removed her bottle of medicine. All of you inserted cyanide into the bottle, and Mrs. Baynes replaced it in her room. Later that night, Lady Giselle consumed some of the medicine, and it killed her. That is what happened, and therefore I am arresting all of you on the charge of murder."

The looks of apprehension had changed to fear, bordering on panic. However, Mrs. Baynes spoke up.

"How wonderfully amusing, Inspector. Such a fine imagination you and your detective must have. You have no proof whatsoever of what you are saying, and other than denying everything you have said, none of us will say anything further without having our barristers and solicitors present, will we."

Her last two words were directed to the other four, and they took the hint and volubly agreed.

"A wise move, of course," said Lestrade. "So, while you are waiting for your lawyers to arrive. I shall put an offer on the table. You don't have to say anything, but I expect that one of you will. You see, we have a witness to what you did who is prepared to inform the court that the account I just gave you is true."

"Impossible!" said Bentley Baynes. "The maid is dead, and we had nothing to do with that either."

"Thank you, Mr. Baynes," said Lestrade. "I am well aware that the maid, who likely witnessed what took place, is dead. I'm not talking about her."

Again, there was a moment of stunned silence before Jefferson Vanderstone muttered an oath and added, "The groom, Private Burnt Face, right? He's not credible. You cannot get a conviction in any court based on the report of a pathetic wreck of a crippled soldier."

"Well now," said Lestrade, "you may be right. Having you all hanged for murder would be difficult to obtain. But conspiracy to commit murder … well now, that might be easier. And as those are both serious charges, you would all be denied bail and stuck in jail until your case comes to court in a year or so, and then if you are convicted of conspiracy, you could be sent away for life or, more likely, at least ten years. But that would be a lot of work for us, and so we're making an offer."

"What?" said Baynes.

"One of you is going to confess here and now before your lawyers arrive. Whoever speaks up first will be considered a witness for the Crown, charged only with aiding after the fact, and will most likely get off with a stiff fine. So there. Who is going to take the offer? First one to speak wins. The rest of you lose."

For two very long minutes, there was complete silence in the room. At first, the five of them glanced at each other, waiting to see if one of them would take Lestrade up on his offer. None said a word. Slowly, smug smiles spread across their faces as they realized that they were not going to betray each other and would form a solid phalanx to fight their accuser.

"A brave try, Inspector," said Mrs. Baynes, "but you failed. And now I shall place a phone call to our lawyers, and we shall wait in silence until they arrive, won't we?"

Again, her last two words were issued as a command to the other four, and all the heads nodded.

"There is something," said Holmes, "that you all appear to be forgetting. If one of you confesses and the other four all go to jail, the court will award control of all of the shares of the Fidelity and Empire Trading and Investments Company Limited to the one who assisted the Crown, and the rest of you will end up with—"

"I win! I confess!" shouted Cuthbert Molesworth, and he leapt to his feet, sending his chair toppling over behind him. "It all happened precisely as you said, Inspector. We all agreed that the bitch would have to go."

"Why you stinking little turd," bellowed Baynes. "We will get you for—oww!"

He jerked as if in pain, and I guessed that his wife had delivered a quick kick to his ankle under the table. Her sharp rebuke of, "Shut up, you fool," confirmed my suspicion.

Molesworth carried on. "You're right Bentley, I am, and I confess that I brought the test tube and gave every one of us enough to kill her, and we all tapped it into her elixir bottle. We agreed to blame it on Dr. Quack, and the only thing that did not go according to our conspired plan was her catching wind of what we were up to and running off to see Sherlock Holmes. But then she conveniently died whilst there."

Lestrade rose from his chair and, in a very officious tone, announced that the four of them were under arrest for murder and conspiracy to commit murder and was about to conclude his charge when Molesworth interrupted him.

"Not so fast, Inspector. You and your famous detective are missing something."

Chapter Twenty-One

In One Big Gulp

 hat?" said Lestrade.

"The murder weapon," said Molesworth, smirking.

"We don't need it."

"Oh, but you would have a much stronger case if you had it." Molesworth had departed from his place at the table and stepped behind Mrs. Vanderstone. "And here it is."

He quickly leaned down to the floor, grabbed Mrs. Vanderstone's handbag and retreated to his place.

"Give that back to me!" she screamed.

"In a moment, my dear cousin. First, let us see what is in it."

He tipped up the handbag and slowly let the contents roll out onto the table. The bag was full of bottles of pills, small tins of ointments, handkerchiefs and cosmetics and one large test tube, plugged with a cork stopper.

"After the deed was done," said Molesworth, "I gave the murder weapon to this lady whose capacious handbag was padded sufficiently to protect it and all of her other assorted medications."

"Bring that to me," said Lestrade.

"As you wish, sir. But first, you really should confirm what is in it, shouldn't you?"

He undid the stopper and tapped a generous ounce of the beige powder into the palm of his hand. Then he walked over to Sherlock Holmes and extended his hand under Holmes's face. Holmes instinctively pulled his head back from the poison.

"Relax, Mr. Holmes. I am not going to hurt anyone now that I have the Crown looking after me. Here, take a sniff. Is it or is it not cyanide powder?"

Holmes locked his right hand onto Molesworth's wrist and slowly brought the open palm under his nose.

"It's cyanide. There's enough in your hand and left in the test tube to kill a dozen people."

"Do you really think so?" said Molesworth. "then watch as it kills just one."

Everyone in the room gasped in horror as he slapped his palm against his open mouth. Mrs. Vanderstone screamed, and her husband shouted at him. He just smiled and reached for the still-full cup of tea in front of him and took a gulp.

His action was met with terrified silence.

"Nothing to say, my dears? I've just murdered myself in front of you, and you're not even going to say goodbye?"

No one spoke, and we waited for him to start to writhe in pain and foam at the mouth.

Nothing happened. He just stood there smiling.

"Oops. I'm still alive. Dear me, what happened? Nobody making a guess? I'll just have to tell you. There was no cyanide in the test tube. It was powdered almonds. Harmless. My little ruse to prove that all of you were ready to kill Giselle, and you cooperated wonderfully."

"What in the devil are you trying to do here?" snapped Lestrade. "A murder investigation is not a game. Now explain yourself."

"I am an author. Not yet a famous one but on my way. I have written the history of this utterly despicable and evil family, and my climax is having them all try to kill poor Lady Giselle."

"Don't be absurd," said Lestrade.

"Not at all, Inspector. I assure you that my draft of this event is already in the hands of my agent, Mr. Vincent Woolens. His office is on Exeter Street. You can find a copy of the text there. He assured me he could give it to Mr. Herbert Smith at the *Strand,* and he would love to publish it in installments alongside Dr. Watson's accounts of the adventures of Sherlock Holmes. Of course, I shall have to alter a few details of the events, as they unfolded in a somewhat different manner than I had predicted, but the entire awful story of this family with its despicable history in transporting slaves and smuggling is going to be fully revealed. And now I shall be not only a rich writer, but I will take over the family estate. For even if the almonds were harmless, they all did conspire to murder Giselle."

"Why you vile little traitor," said Bentley Baynes. His fists were clenched. He started to rise from his chair, and he appeared ready to batty-fang Cuthbert Molesworth. Once again, his progress was impeded by an obvious kick to his ankle. His wife forcibly held him in his place whilst she herself stood up.

"Bravo!" she cried as she started to clap her hands together vigorously. "Bravo Cuthbert. You win the prize for the best game of the weekend. I haven't had such a good time at games in my life. Well done. Of course, we all knew it was just one of your wonderful games, didn't we?"

Yet again, her final two words were directed to the others at the table. Her husband and Mr. Vanderstone looked utterly clueless for several seconds and then burst into applause as well.

"Jolly good!" shouted Vanderstone. "Bang up the elephant," chimed in Bentley Baynes, who had managed to discern what his much-more-clever wife was cheering about.

"We all won," Estelle Baynes added with a less-than-genuine laugh. "Well, all except our dull inspector and his disappointed detective. Poor chaps. Now what are they going to do? We were just playing another game, but there's a nasty murderer still out there. So, back to work, boys. Maybe it was the doctor, after all. Meaning no offense to Doctor Watson, but these medical types have been known to kill their patients."

The rest of them affected cheers, and the two men came over to Molesworth and gave him a congratulatory pat on the back, somewhat more forcefully applied than is usual among teammates.

Without asking, they all filed out of the dining room. The last to leave, Bentley Baynes, looked back at us. "Unless you are planning to arrest us for conspiring to play a game, you have no reason to be in this house any longer. Kindly vacate the premises ... now."

Lestrade, Holmes and I looked at each other, baffled and deflated.

Chapter Twenty-Two

Jack Tar Knows All

"Correct me if I am wrong, Inspector," said Holmes, "but I believe that our presence here can no longer be justified."

"Having made your grand announcement and accused them all and then made to look like a fool, I'd say you're right," replied Lestrade. "And having hauled me over so early on a Sunday morning before I had my breakfast, I'd say we should make our way back out to the High Street and find something to eat. I'm sure I will be somewhat less testy when I am no longer hungry."

Within fifteen minutes, the constables had been relieved of their duties and sent back to their station, and Lestrade, Holmes and I found a café on Avenue Road. After a silent devouring of a full English, Holmes sat back and lit a cigarette.

"While it now appears that the lot of them may have conspired to kill Giselle, they did not succeed. However, someone did, and it remains possible that it was one of them. Probably, the same person killed the maid after she witnessed the murder. Their reaction of the lot of them on being told of the death of Giselle was clearly feigned with amateur acting. Only Molesworth seemed genuinely surprised. The others were not. However, their stunned silence on learning of the death of the maid did seem authentic. Whoever killed her was clever enough to pretend to be shocked along with the rest of them."

"If it truly was one of them," said Lestrade, "but that does not give me anyone to arrest, now does it? Or do I have to go back to the doctor? Or maybe the racehorse owners? Or the shipping crew who were put out of business by Giselle."

Holmes took another slow puff on his cigarette. "An excellent suggestion, Inspector. Our next stop should be the docklands. If Lord Vanderstone was involved in illegal activities decades ago, there may be a reason we cannot imagine why someone might want him as well as his daughter dead."

"Then you can go there," said Lestrade. "It's a Sunday morning of the August Bank Holiday, and I have better things to do. Let me know when you're ready to send me to make another arrest, and see if you can do better next time."

Even on a Sunday morning, when the streets of London were bereft of traffic, it still took us nearly an hour to travel from Primrose Hill to Limehouse. Holmes directed the cab driver to go to an address on Narrow Street, a part of London that, even on a Sunday morning, was not wise to be in when well-dressed and without a weapon. It was the same part of the city in which I had, long ago, hauled Holmes out of an opium den, and I was not particularly thrilled to be back in it.

The pub at which we stopped, *The Grapes,* was somewhat infamous. The novelist, Charles Dickens had disguised it with the name, *The Six Jolly Fellowship Porters,* and, in a less-than-complimentary manner, accurately described it as:

a tavern of a dropsical appearance, long settled down into a state of hale infirmity. In its whole constitution it had not a straight floor, and hardly a straight line. Externally, it was a narrow lopsided wooden jumble of corpulent windows heaped one upon another as you might heap as many toppling oranges, with a crazy wooden verandah impending over the water.

It was patronized by the vast multitudes from the docklands, the sailors, stevedores, laborers, barge owners, prostitutes, and procurers who lived their entire lives in the demi-world of East London. Fortunately for us, there were only a few patrons present late on a Sunday morning, but even those few looked on us with unvarnished hostility when we entered.

"Holmes, what are we doing *here?*"

"Recruiting sailors."

Before I had time to query his reply, the barkeep approached our table.

"Good morning there, gents. Haven't seen the two of you here before. What brings you in?"

"Two pints of cider," said Holmes, "and some information."

"The cider, I can do. The information depends."

"My good man," said Holmes, "I am seeking a sailor, but a very specific man. Ideally, he will have spent his life sailing from England to the seven seas, will now be too old to ever be hired again. But he will know everything there is to know about every ship and every shipping company that sails from the port of London. Might you direct me to such a man?"

"I might."

"I am more than willing to pay a fair wage to such a man, perhaps a full day's wage for only a few minutes of his time. Can you help me, sir?"

"I can."

"And will you?"

"I will."

"Excellent. Then to what address in this neighborhood will you send me to find such a man?"

"You can go straight away to 76 Narrow Street and ask for Jack. He's your man."

"Thank you, sir," said Holmes, and he started to rise from his chair, leaving his cider untouched, but then he stopped.

"You're having me on," he said to the barkeep. "That is the address of this pub."

"That it is, and the old sailor sitting over there by the wall is Jack. Full name, at least what he calls himself now, is Jack Tar. You can take your cider with you. No reason to leave it behind."

We looked over to the wall and the elderly man who was sitting at a table by himself, sipping on a cup of tea and nibbling a cheese sandwich. If I were to judge his age by his face, I would have been compelled to say he was one-hundred and fifty years old. His leathery skin was deeply cut with crevasses and highlighted with a few blotches of white where cancer of the skin must have afflicted him decades ago. Even at midday on a late summer afternoon, he was wearing a roll-top sweater and a navy-blue coat.

We walked over to him and pulled up chairs to his table.

"Good morning, sir," said Holmes. "Might we have a word with you, sir? It is Mr. Jack Tar, is it not?" He spoke loudly and clearly, assuming that the old chap was likely hard of hearing

He looked first at Holmes and then at me with eyes that were once clear but had glossed over years ago.

"I heard what you said to Tom. Don't shout at me. What do you want, and what's it worth to you?"

Holmes extracted a pound note from his wallet and put it on the table. Jack smirked.

"That'll do. Whatever you want to know must be either important or illegal. Maybe both. So haul anchor and get underway. And don't be talking to me like I'm addle-brained. I may be old, but I'm no chowder-head."

"Most certainly, you are not, sir, else Tom would not have recommended you. And I assure you, sir, there is nothing illegal in our need of your help. In truth, it may help to solve a crime. My name, sir, is—"

"I know who you are. You're Sherlock Holmes. Blimey if I haven't read all those stories about you. Nothing better to do with my time these days, so may as well read about you as waste my time sitting here for hours. And you," he said, looking at me. "must be the doctor who writes all that nonsense. That right, mate?"

"It is, but I confess, I'm not much of a mate. My only time at sea was—"

"Out to Afghanistan and back. Right? That's what I read. You sailed home on the *Orentes*. Right? But your friend here is a total landlubber. Right? Well then, speak up. What do you want to know?"

"We need to know, sir," said Holmes, "about ships and shipping lines that might, from time to time, carry cargo that is not what you might call totally legal."

"There's a half-dozen of them that sail every day out of London and many more from Liverpool and Southampton. Can you not be more specific? I haven't got all day."

"To be specific, sir, what can you tell us about ships that used to carry slaves well after the banning of the slave trade and, to be specific, any of those ships or their owners, that today are shipping indentured workers from Africa, Asia, and India?"

"England ended the slave trade in 1807. The British Navy enforced it. No honest captain shipped slaves after that," said the man who called himself Jack Tar.

"But what about the dishonest ones?"

"They kept it up until 1867. Took slaves to America until 1860 and to Cuba and Brazil for seven years after that. Ran the business from New York and Boston. Registered their ships under the American flag so that the Royal Navy wouldn't board and seize them. But then they ran into Abe Lincoln."

"You mean the emancipation and amendment he brought about."

"No. Those were just pieces of paper. I mean a bloke was caught in New York running slaves, and instead of getting a slap on the wrist, Lincoln had him hanged. That put an end to that nonsense."

"Is that so? Well now, our particular concern is with ships and shipping lines that moved from the slave trade into transport of indentured laborers. What can you tell us about them?"

For an awkwardly long interval, the old sailor fixed Holmes with a stare of two dark, clouded eyes.

"What you are asking, Mr. Detective, is about Reece Vanderstone, and you want to know if he was murdered. That's what you're after, isn't it?"

"In part, yes, it is."

"Then what's the other part?"

"His daughter, Lady Giselle Vanderstone, has also been murdered."

The weathered old face took on a look of unfeigned surprise.

"They killed the girl too? Aye, that is a surprise. Mind you, the only real surprise is that she didn't kill them first. She was a shark if ever there was one. Pretty as a puffin, but as deadly as a great white."

"Was she now? Can you tell me who might have wanted her dead?"

"That I don't know. Only rumors. Mind you, if I did know, I wouldn't tell you."

"Oh, and why not?" asked Holmes.

"Because, if I did, both of us might find ourselves hanged from the yardarm before dawn tomorrow. You'll have to go ask elsewhere if you want to take that risk."

"And where might I ask? Can you tell me that?"

"Reece and before him, Old Basil, his father—he was one damned son of a bitch if there ever was one—they did all their trading business with the British and African Shipping Line. It's run now by Elder and Dempster."

"And where might I find them, sir?"

"They have an office on the East India Dock Road. Either Elder or Dempster will be there."

"On a Sunday?" I asked.

"Doctors can take Sundays off. Sailors can't. Nobody bothered to tell the winds and the tides that it was the Sabbath."

Chapter Twenty-Three

In Ship Shape

The office of the Elder Dempster Shipping Line was in a nondescript dirty-yellow brick building at the corner of Canton Street and the East India Dock Road. A brass plaque on the door indicated we were at their London office and gave the address of the head office in Clydeside, Glasgow. We entered, and I observed a room with several desks and a utilitarian décor. Not a farthing had been spent on anything that might have added a mote of taste.

Except for a young clerk at one of the desks, there was nobody present. The fellow looked up at us and appeared surprised.

"Good day, gentlemen," he said, with a thick Glasgow accent. "The office is not open today. Would you mind coming back tomorrow? Auch, make that Tuesday, as tomorrow is the Bank Holiday."

"We need to speak with either Mr. Elder or Mr. Dempster," said Holmes. "It is quite urgent. I assume that one of them is present."

"Mr. Elder is in Glasgow, and Mr. Dempster cannot be disturbed. If you leave your card, I shall tell him you called in, and he can see you on Tuesday. Do have a good day, gentlemen."

"Of course," said Holmes. "Here is my card. Please tell Mr. Dempster that Sherlock Holmes wished to speak with him concerning the untimely death of Lady Giselle Vanderstone."

Judging by the look on his face, that got the clerk's attention. He stood up, walked over to us and took Holmes's card.

"Please wait here," he said and vanished up the staircase. He returned less than a minute later.

"Mr. Dempster would very much like to speak to you. Please follow me."

He led us to the upper floor of the building and along a hallway that could have used a fresh coat of paint and into a small office that looked out over the East India Road. A casually dressed man of an age somewhere in his sixties was standing and waiting for us. He had a ruddy complexion and a head of thinning hair that was likely glowing red in his youth and had now faded to some shade between dull orange and beige. His torso still passed for the lean footballer he must have been forty years earlier.

"Do come in, gentlemen," he said. "The news you bring here is deeply disturbing, and I would be grateful for a full report."

He spoke in a staccato rhythm and thick brogue that identified him as a southern Scot. My ability to identify accents was nowhere near that of Holmes, but I would have guessed he was from either the Borders or Dumfriesshire.

He gestured to a small table surrounded by hardback chairs at which he wished us to sit and then spoke to his clerk. "Andrew, a pot of tea and a plate of shortbread for our visitors."

As soon as we are seated facing him, he gave Holmes a hard look.

"What happened?"

"Lady Vanderstone was murdered," said Holmes.

Mr. Dempster closed his eyes and quietly shook his head. "I am very sorry to hear that," he said almost in a whisper.

"Although," said Holmes, "you do not appear to be shocked or even terribly surprised."

"Those who live by the sword … auch, you as like dinna ken, do you, else you would not be here asking questions. Well, what do you know happened?"

"She was poisoned to death early Saturday morning. As she conducted extensive business with your firm, we are hoping that you might tell us all you know about her and thus help us apprehend her killer. Is it correct that she recently terminated her contracts with your shipping line?"

Mr. John Dempster paused before answering and nodded slowly. "Aye and no. She came in here a fortnight ago, and we had a meeting. It was agreed that the decision to stop working together would be announced as mutually determined. In truth, we put an end to it, explained our reasons, and she agreed. If you see a connection between what happened here and her death, then pose your questions. We've naught to hide. But I can tell you, right off, she had many enemies."

"So we have learned," said Holmes, "and we are investigating all of them. Would you be so kind as to explain to me the nature of her commerce with your firm and your reason for ending it. You might also give me the names of any who were her enemies."

"Her enemies? Aye, that's a long list. She might have been a skinny malinky long legs, but she was as bonnie a lassie as I ever met. Any man would like to believe that such a lovely woman would be sweet and charming as well, but she used her tongue like a Maxim gun. Cut a man to ribbons if he dared to argue with her. So, making a list of those who hated her would not be much use. You could add the name of every boffin she met and had words with."

"We are aware she had a sharp tongue," said Holmes, "but if that alone were cause to being murdered, there would be many fewer women in England. There must have been other reasons as well."

"Have ye met the rest of her family?"

"We have, and they are all possible suspects, but we need to explore every possibility, every connection in her life. Would you mind answering my question? What was the nature of your business with her?"

"With us? Shipping, it was. Started many years ago with her father. We sent   goods to Africa and across to the Americas."

"Did that include slaves?"

"Aye, it did. But that ended years ago. When that ended, Reece went into sending coolies, and peons and Africans all over the world to work the fields. Not a pleasant line of cargo but not against any law either. And good money in it. Lady Giselle could have kept it up after Reece fell off his horse and died. We're still doin' it today, but she got out of it."

"If it was legal and profitable, why did she stop? Did she develop moral scruples?"

"Morals? Her? No, she couldn't afford to have morals. Neither could you if you were as rich as she was."

"Then why?"

"Because we agreed that neither of us wanted to end up getting hanged."

"For what?"

"It's called treason. Reece also had a contract with King Leopold to send boatloads of arms to his army in the Congo Free State," said Dempster.

"That may have been morally questionable, but it is not treason."

"No, but it becomes that when you take those shipments around the Horn and drop them off in Lourenço Marques."

"Pray, go on."

"When the war in the Cape started up, Her Majesty required two of our ships, the *Monterey* and the *Montezuma,* to take troops from England to Capetown or Durban. Auch, then didn't Reece start sending all these bales of used clothing to help the wretched mothers and children in Mozambique. Some of the poorest people on earth. That's what could have got us all hanged."

"Sending charity clothing? That makes no sense whatsoever."

"It does when stuffed inside those bales were all manner of rifles and ammunition and even a small cannon or two. From Lourenço Marques, they went by the railway that connects with Pretoria, but they were taken off, and all those arms were handed over to the Boers, Britain's very stubborn enemy."

"Are you telling me that Lord Vanderstone was aiding and abetting the enemy? Why would he do such a thing?"

"His family came over from Holland a few generations back. Their sympathies were with the Boers. So was most of Europe for that matter, including Kaiser Willie, and he's the Queen's grandson."

"And did Lady Giselle put an end to these shipments out of patriotism?"

"Nay, she never had any use for any moral standard. But the lass was smart enough to see that the profit had dwindled and risk was too high to justify the return. When you're sending anything through a warring part of the world, the cost of capital to assemble the shipment goes through the roof. Too much chance the ship will be seized and everything lost. That's why she agreed to put an end to it."

"And you agreed with her?"

"Aye, I did. My three score and ten years are not that far off, and I'd just as soon not have my neck stretched at this point in my life."

"You will have to be more explicit, Mr. Dempster," said Holmes. "Why would her actions lead to anyone wanting to murder her?"

"I'll wager that the Boers weren't too happy about it. They lost their reliable shipments of arms. Had they been kept up, goodness knows, they might have won the war."

"That is a possibility, although somewhat remote. Who else lost as a result of the cessation of the shipments?"

"The arms manufacturers and dealers. Those shipments were valuable."

"The sale of arms to foreign countries," said Holmes, "is one of the largest and most lucrative components of international commerce. Whatever was smuggled to the Boers would hardly be missed. If necessary, the Boers would have found other channels. Is there no one else?"

"The banks who were providing the capital and charging twenty-five percent interest. They were making a fortune," said Dempster.

"That, sir, is what banks do."

"Aye, it is, but do you no want to ask me the name of the bank that was providing all the capital and collecting all the profit?"

"It hardly matters. Every bank is as greedy and as ruthless as the next one. But very well, if you insist. Which bank were they using?"

"It's called the London and South America Bank. They have offices in the City, on Gresham Street."

Chapter Twenty-Four

Hypothetically Speaking

As soon as we were done with Mr. Dempster and his shipping line, we hailed a cab to take us yet again to the Vanderstone home in Primrose Hill, and I directed the driver to take us by way of the Strand.

Holmes had disappeared into his thoughts, but my mind had turned to the unfortunate fate of the family.

"Rather a bitter irony, wouldn't you say, Holmes? The father was shipping arms to the Boers, and they could have been using those very rifles and artillery to attack and kill his son and his squad."

"The sins of the fathers are indeed visited upon the children, Watson. It has been ever thus."

"And on the step-children?"

"Until now, no. They have gotten away. That is about to end."

"What do you suppose happened?"

"It is my guess that Lord Vanderstone thought it clever to steer a significant portion of income in the form of interest to his step-sons by using the bank at which they were employed."

"You think maybe they were gaining from that?"

"I am certain of it. There are a hundred other banks he could have used. Jefferson Vanderstone and Bentley Baynes would receive a healthy commission for bringing the business to their bank. It was yet another clever scheme they found for substantially enriching the family without creating any new product or service. They are exactly the type of bankers that give capitalism a bad name and provide fodder for the Fabians."

"Substantially enough to lead to murder?"

"That is what we are about to find out."

When the cab reached the intersection of Burleigh Street and the Strand, I called up to the driver to stop.

"What are you doing?" asked Holmes.

"Just a quick stop to have a chat with Herb Smith. I'll be back straight away."

"Watson, I do not have—"

"Patience, Holmes. It has to do with this case. You should be glad I thought of it."

I was back in the cab in ten minutes and feeling quite pleased with myself.

"I presume that all had to do with Cuthbert Molesworth," said Holmes.

"It did indeed. I advised the editor that anything he received from Mr. Molesworth would inevitably be full of falsehoods and leave the Strand liable for lawsuits. He thanked me and sends his warmest regards to you."

"A rather severe way to administer justice to a struggling young writer."

"It is, but I have no use for writers who contrive to manipulate events for the sole purpose of being able to write about them."

"Well done, Watson. Of course, if you were to take your chastising to its logical end, would you not have to put half the reporters and newspapers of Fleet Street out of business?"

"We all have to do our bit."

By the time we returned to Primrose Hill, it was early afternoon on the Sunday of a sunny holiday weekend. The early autumn flowers—the Chrysanthemums, begonias, asters and a few tall sunflowers— were all in fine display in the well-tended garden beds. On the manicured lawn, the two couples were engaging in a game of croquet and appeared to be enjoying themselves. Cuthbert Molesworth was noticeable by his absence.

Standing at the ready to meet their whims was a young woman in a maid's uniform. I did not remember seeing her before and concluded that she must be the rapid replacement for the recently deceased Miss Gladys Fealy.

The game stopped as the cab pulled up to the door, and we stepped out. We were greeted by a bellicose bellow from Bentley Baynes.

"Go home, Holmes! Can't you see we are busy with much more important matters?"

Holmes ignored him and started walking directly toward the middle of the wickets, rendering the game impossible to continue.

"So sorry, Mr. Holmes," shouted Jefferson Vanderstone, "but we do not conduct business on the Sabbath. You will have to return on Tuesday."

"My ox has fallen into a ditch," said Holmes. "I am here on behalf of Scotland Yard, and we are continuing our investigation. This will not take long. Please meet me in the parlor in five minutes. You can return to your game later."

"Who says we have to?" said Baynes. "What if we just tell you to go home, Holmes?"

He laughed at the repetition of his supposed wit, and his brother-in-law joined in.

"Then I shall call for the police wagons, and you will be taken to the Embankment for further questioning. It is your choice," replied Holmes.

Grudgingly, they put down their mallets and sauntered slowly back into the house. All four of them announced that they required a visit to the lavatory and took their time about appearing in the parlor.

Whilst we were waiting, I said hello to the new maid. It would be an understatement to say that she was attractively endowed and more than somewhat on the voluptuous side. I introduced myself and asked, "Is this your first day here?"

"Very nice to meet you, Dr. Watson. My name is Angel, and yes, sir, I started this morning."

"Which agency referred you?"

"None, sir. I've never had no opportunity to work in service before. I was working 'til yesterday at the Duke of York. It's only a few blocks away on St. Ann's Terrace."

"Well, good on you," I said. "How came you by this position?"

"Mr. Baynes, sir. He comes in all the time, and he's always friendly. Last night he came by late and chatted with me, and offered me this situation. I'm earning two times more than I was in the pub. He's a very kind man to me."

"I'm sure he is."

Mr. and Mrs. Vanderstone entered the room and sat on the sofa. Mrs. Vanderstone sneezed twice and quickly reached into her handbag and brought out a bottle that I assumed was Dr. Anderson's *Allergy Alleviator,* pulled open the stopper and took a swallow. I refrained from offering the common-sense medical advice avoiding hours outdoors amidst flowers, grasses and shrubs would be a far more effective way to reduce her allergic reactions than swallowing gallons of some concoction that, going by its red color, was likely ninety-five percent Campari.

Mr. and Mrs. Baynes joined them on an adjacent sofa. Mrs. Baynes looked over to her sister-in-law and feigned a smile.

"I do hope, Constance, that this annoying Mr. Holmes will not waste too much of our time. We have far more important things to attend to. My ball was touching yours when we left the pitch, and I am about to give you a good, hard smack halfway to Marylebone."

"Why, Estelle, you mean, nasty girl you. Just you wait until it's my turn and send your ball flying all the way to Camden Town."

They both broke into gales of laughter, and Mrs. Baynes looked at Holmes.

"Please get on with whatever questions you have, Mr. Holmes. We do not have all day to waste with you. Any intelligent man can see that Giselle was murdered—in your front room, I would remind you—by someone who was not involved in Cuthbert's little game. And as to the maid, I hear she was sniffing herself into happy oblivion when her overworked heart up and quit pushing blood through her oversized body. So, Mr. Holmes, what is it now?"

"My questions, Madam," said Holmes, "shall not be directed to you as I am quite certain there is nothing of use to me that you can say. I shall ask my questions of your husband and brother-in-law."

"Gentlemen," he said, looking at Vanderstone and Baynes, "allow me to confirm that the two of you work at the Bank of London and South America on Gresham Street. Is that correct?"

"Oh, dear me," said Jefferson Vanderstone, "I suppose that is the name of it, is it not Bentley?"

"It is, but I would hardly say that we *work* there." The other three guffawed, and he continued. "At least, I don't, and I must say I just cannot remember the last time I saw you actually *working*." There were more guffaws.

"So, *no,* Mr. Holmes, neither Bentley nor I work there, although from time to time we do put in an appearance. Bentley, my dear chap, I do believe I saw you there twice last week."

"And that was once more than you, Jeff, old boy."

Both of them slapped their thighs in laughter. Holmes was about to say something, but Mrs. Baynes spoke first.

"Unless you want to continue to waste our time, Mr. Holmes, I suggest you not ask stupid questions to which you are bound to receive a stupid answer. My husband told you yesterday that they both worked there. Why can you not ask an intelligent question?"

"From time to time, madam," said Holmes, "I have reason to doubt the probity of the data I am told by certain people, and it is necessary to re-confirm. I'm sure you face the same problem often. But allow me then to ask a question to which I was not told an answer yesterday. Were the two of you responsible for bringing to your bank the accounts that dealt with all of the business carried on between the Fidelity and Empire Trading and Investments Company Limited and the British and African Line, now doing business as Elder Dempster Shipping? Is that correct?"

"Elder and who?" said Vanderstone, feigning a puzzled look. "What say, Bentley, does he mean those two Scottish blokes. Here I thought their names were Haggis MacBagpipe and Crotchity MacCrabb."

"Well, garn, I dinna never ken, did you? Aye, Mr. MacHolmes, those are the two porridge wogs what runs the ships," replied his brother-in-law. Both men guffawed some more.

"How much," said Holmes, "are you paid every month as a commission on the income your bank earns from the business conducted between your bank and the family firm?"

"Oh, come, come, Mr. Holmes, really?" said Jefferson Vanderstone. "A gentleman never discusses his income, and a gentleman never asks."

"An excellent point, sir," said Holmes, "and I trust I have not offended Mrs. Baynes by asking yet another question to which I already know the answer. Oh, does that surprise you? Then kindly permit me to state the amount of your current monthly income. It is zero. Yes, not a farthing. But a few months ago, it was in excess of a thousand pounds, wasn't it? So, without being ungentlemanly and discussing your current income, kindly explain to me what happened to it. Where did it go?"

First Vanderstone started to say something and then stopped. Baynes looked as if he were about to speak and said nothing. Both of them looked at Estelle Baynes, and she gave a short shake of her head at both of them and then smiled sweetly at Holmes.

"In business, Mr. Holmes, you have good times and bad times. Anyone who has ever worked a day in the City knows that. We are currently experiencing a quarter of negative growth. And it means little or nothing. True men of commerce don't whinge. Do you?"

"I might," replied Holmes, "if I were to discover that my stepsister sister was the one who put an end to my income. That is what happened, is it not? Lady Giselle discovered that you two were making a fortune first off of running arms to the enemy and then by transporting indentured workers in conditions no better than your step-father and his father transported slaves back before 1867. I might be exceptionally angry with her and quite prepared to get rid of her. In truth, gentlemen, you appear to have had an excellent motive for committing murder."

"Now you look here," said Baynes, "I don't happen to like what I think you're accusing me of and—oww!"

He glanced at his wife, who firmly laid her hand on his forearm and likely applied her boot to his ankle.

"My dear Mr. Holmes," she said, ignoring her husband, "I'm so sorry, but you have it all wrong. For the past three years, the firm was run by Giselle and her father. Bentley and Jefferson had little or nothing to do with it other than trying to help Lord Vanderstone secure the necessary capital. But when he died, they had no choice but to become more involved. They discovered the shipments Giselle and Reece had been sending throughout the war. They became aware that shipments of arms were still being sent to both sides of every conflict on earth. Rifles and ammunition were going to the rebels fighting our soldiers in Nigeria, to the Haitians fighting the Germans in Haiti, to the Siamese rising up against the French in

Siam, and to the Macedonians who were trying to get rid of the Turks. Isn't that right?"

She spoke her last question to her husband and brother-in-law, and again, it was more of a command.

"Right, right, yes, yes, right, of course, right," the two men babbled back.

"My husband and my brother stepped in and put an end to all of that. In doing so, they incurred a serious drop in their income. Their actions were nothing but sacrificial and were done in the name of Great Britain. It is a shame that Giselle decided to end up dead on your sofa, Mr. Holmes, otherwise you could have put her under oath and forced her to admit the truth of everything I've just told you."

"Oh," chimed in Mrs. Vanderstone, "the little vixen might have denied it, but we all knew how easily she could lie through her teeth. Isn't that right?' She aped her sister-in-law's example of delivering the imperative disguised as the interrogative.

"If," said Holmes, "you were, hypothetically speaking of course, accused of murdering her, is it not highly likely that a jury would be more likely to believe in your ruthless greed and not your patriotic altruism? Given the substantial income you lost, would the two of you not have an irresistible motive to make sure that her bottle of medicine was deadly?"

"If we are speaking hypothetically, Mr. Holmes," replied Mrs. Baynes immediately, "may we also consider the situation in which England's most famous detective truly believes that our claim to have been playing a game and not conspiring to poison Lady Giselle was false. May we also, hypothetically speaking, accept the possibility that he is indeed quite certain that we all did conspire to kill her. May we entertain such a hypothesis, Mr. Holmes?"

I was not at all sure where this devious woman was going with her questions and, from the look on Holmes's face, neither was he. Nevertheless, he nodded.

"Yes, madam, we can consider that possibility. I may even be predisposed to accept its truth."

"Ah, are you now? Well then, if so, you would, of necessity, have to also conclude that my husband and my brother are the stupidest men on earth."

Bentley Baynes looked quite insulted by his wife's assertion. Clearly, he had no idea what she was up to either.

"Well, do you, Mr. Holmes?" she said. "Are they the stupidest men on earth?"

"Stupid is not amongst the adjectives I would use to describe them, no."

"Nor would I. But I regret to inform you that you cannot have it both ways. You cannot believe that they did indeed conspire to murder Giselle by participating in Cuthbert's cooperative poisoning plan *and* then be so stupid as to think they had to murder her twice. So, which is it, Mr. Holmes? Do you believe that we all conspired to kill her and thought we were doing so by cooperating with Cuthbert? I am quite certain, Mr. Holmes, that that is what you, in truth, do believe to be true. Don't you?"

Holmes said nothing, and she carried on. "Yes, you do. We all know that you do. Then the only way you can accuse the two men of subsequently acting independently is if you believe them to be imbecilic fools, which you know is false. I rest my case, Mr. Holmes. Once again, you have lost. And if you will now excuse us, we have an exciting game of croquet to finish. Good day, Mr. Holmes."

Using her chin as a directional signal, she indicated that the other three were to follow her out of the room and back to the croquet game.

Chapter Twenty-Five

Filed Away

olmes did not get up. He lit a cigarette, sat back in his chair and scowled.

"A penny for your thoughts," I said, sensing that he was descending into anger.

He looked up at me with a blank stare and then forced a thin smile. "Thank you, my friend, for your efforts to cheer me up, but expressing my thoughts would most likely allow my feelings to emerge and cloud my reasoning."

"Very well then, a penny for your reasonings, your scientific observations, if you insist."

"My highly unscientific observation is that I have seldom met a family that is so utterly devoid of any moral sentiments. The sky above them is vacant. Whatever gods might once have imbued the household with decency have departed."

"Then perhaps it is time that we departed as well. A stroll back home through the park would do wonders for your spirits. Shall we go?"

"Not yet. All of the documents and items of interest the constables assembled in the library are still laid out. I shall return to them and see if there is anything I can see that will lead to a reasonable conclusion. From there, I may be able to assemble an accusation that will not falter on the rocks of that woman's devious arguments. You go on home if you wish. Tell Mrs. Hudson I shall be there in time for supper."

"I'm in no rush. I don't mind sitting and writing up my notes whilst you comb through the mounds of papers and what not. It is possible that an insight will descend upon you, and you might find my presence as a sounding board useful."

"That is highly unlikely, but your thoughtfulness is appreciated."

He rose from his chair and, with yet another cigarette in hand, walked slowly back to the library. As he was passing through the door, he stopped and stood still, gazing into the room.

"What's wrong," I said from behind him, not being able to see past him.

"It has all been cleaned up and put away."

His comment was responded to by a woman's voice from one of the bookshelf alcoves.

"I'm glad you noticed," said Miss Holling. "This is the room in which I shall have to work for the rest of the week, and I deplore a mess. I have put everything back where it belongs. It took me all morning, so if there is anything you wish to look at, just tell me, and I shall let you know where to find it."

I sighed inwardly, assuming that Holmes would become even more frustrated and glum. To my surprise, he lifted his head and moved it around, looking back and forth over the room. All of the files and personal effects the constables had brought to us were gone. The tables and desk had been dusted down, the windows and draperies were open, and the place was bright and sunny and full of fresh air.

"An orderly office and library indicate an orderly mind. Thank you, madam, for taking on that chore. Above and beyond the call of duty."

"Not quite sure what my duties are these days, and I do not expect to be here much longer. But as long as I am, I shall try to justify my wages and be useful."

"Would you mind my asking how you knew where each item was to be filed?"

"It was not difficult. I read every one of them and made a decision. I am familiar with all the affairs and machinations of the estate and the firm, so I put things where they clearly belonged."

"Wonderful. A job well done. Would you then be so kind as to answer a few of my questions concerning what you read and observed. It will save me having to spend the same hours to repeat all the reading you have just completed."

"Ask away, Mr. Holmes." She nodded her head, giving her short salt-and-pepper hair a bit of a bounce.

He gestured to her to take the chair behind the massive mahogany desk, and he and I pulled up a couple of hardback chairs to the side across from her.

"If you could, Miss Holling, and I am quite sure you can, would you take a minute or two in your mind and think back over all the documents you read and reviewed here this morning. Take your time. There is no rush. What I would find very useful to know is if there were any items you observed that struck you as being out of order, anomalies, questionable, things that did not make clear sense. I'm sure you know what I mean. So, do take a few minutes and organize them in your mind."

"That won't be necessary."

Her assertion struck me as dismissive of Holmes's request, and he lifted his head and looked surprised and offended.

"I beg your pardon, madam."

"I don't need to sit and think about it. I made a list when I came across something like that before I put it away. No need to waste time thinking it over. I have the list right here."

She pointed to a place on the desk where sat a notepad of the size used by secretaries for taking down dictation. Holmes reached for it, looked at it, and handed it back to her. She smiled at him.

"You are not alone, Mr. Holmes. I have yet to meet a man who could read and write Pitman's shorthand. Shall I read it to you?"

"Please do."

"There's a half-dozen or so items. Several are insignificant. Just some chores that have to be looked after now that Lady Giselle has gone, and I do not expect any of the family will get around to caring about doing them. I'll start with them, shall I?"

"Please do."

"There's a note from Daniel Brock. He was the groom before Othniel. Nice chap. He says that he is still owed one pound, two shillings on his wages. Never had any reason to doubt his honesty, so I'll have to arrange to get that sent to him. The stable master up at the estate in St. Albans is asking if we still need seven hundred pounds of hay sent down every week for the horses we keep here. I'll tell him we do. Wouldn't want those lovely beasts to go hungry. There's a letter to Lord Vanderstone about his son, Clayton. Did you see it?"

"We did."

"Not a nice one to get about your boy, is it. When I put it away, I came across a file with more about his son. He'd been given a list of citations and commendations as long as your arm. Quite the patriotic young man. An estate agent up in St. Albans sent a note to Lady Giselle about putting the property and the house up for sale. She hadn't told me she was thinking about that. Did you know about that?"

"No. We didn't."

"Neither did the rest of the family, I'll wager. A note arrived this morning—Mr. Baynes hasn't seen it yet—from the owner of the

Duke of York pub—saying that Miss Angel Wade—she's the new maid—had signed a contract to work through to the end of December and that he expected compensation from Mr. Baynes for poaching her away. But I can tell you, she'll probably be sent back to him after a month. Bentley the Blowhard tires of his new toys rather quickly."

"But Miss Gladys Fealy had served here for several years, had she not?"

"She had, and for some reason no one knows, he was terrified of her. Mind you, so was Giselle. Don't ask me why. It happened before my time. Well, next on the list is this set of unpaid invoices from Birmingham Small Arms Company, and another from the RSAF in Enfield, and a third from the Eley Brothers up in Edmonton."

"Those are all arms manufacturers," said Holmes.

"That they are, and it looks like someone had put together a rather large shipment of small arms, but there's no telling where they went. Oh, but this might help. There's a telegram from the Liverpool and Manchester Trading Company confirming the items have been shipped."

"To where?"

"Nigeria."

Chapter Twenty-Six

The Logos is in Lagos

hat did they send to Nigeria?" Holmes asked

"It says bales of used clothing," she replied.

"How interesting. Please carry on."

"Whilst putting away some of Lady Giselle's personal invoices, I came across an entire file on the inquest into her stepmother's death. She took her own life. You knew that, I assume."

"We did. However, it is odd that Lady Giselle kept the file. Carry on."

"That's about it, except for all the discrepancies in the bank account records."

"Kindly elucidate."

"It's not a big thing compared to all the money these people have, but every week there's a cash deposit of two hundred pounds and, for the life of me, I have no idea where it comes from. It's odd, that's all."

"It is indeed. Is that the end of your list? Anything else you thought we should know about?"

"Her file box."

"Madam?"

"She kept her private correspondence separate. I assume it might have been letters that had been sent back and forth from lovers or those hapless sods who wanted to be."

"And where is that box?"

"I have it. I keep it under lock and key in my closet. She didn't trust anyone in her family, so she would never leave it around here. However, as I live nearby, she told me I had to keep it for her, and once a week or so she would drop around and put a letter or a file into it."

"Miss Holling, when we came to see you yesterday, you did not say anything about it."

"No, I was upset by the news of her death, and even if I had not been, well, you know what they say—a gentleman never reads another gentleman's mail—the same goes for women. But what with all that has happened, I decided I should tell you about it. If you want, I can bring it around to your office. Baker Street, yes?"

"A penny for *your* thoughts, Watson," said Holmes as we walked back to Baker Street from Primrose Hill.

"They never stopped sending arms. But why Nigeria?" I asked.

"Have you not been following the Press? Britain is at war with the Aro Kingdom. Those poor, benighted people seem to think that they should be able to govern themselves, worship their own god at their own shrine and carry on their own commerce without being told what to do by the almighty British Empire."

"I did see some stories about them. But were they not also enslaving some of the neighboring tribes they conquered?"

"That is what was reported. But our fine soldiers attacked and killed most of them. A very efficient way for the Empire to convince those Africans to behave the way we want them to."

"But that war is over. We won."

"There remains an active insurgency. I suspect that the bales of used clothing were stuffed with Lee-Enfield rifles and ammunition and on their way to give the natives a fighting chance against the Royal Niger Company."

"That would be treason, would it not?"

"It would, and those responsible for it could be tried and hanged."

"So, what does that have to do with the murder of Lady Giselle? Or of the maid?"

"I continue to proceed on the assumption that the maid was an innocent bystander who witnessed the murder of Lady Giselle."

"What do you make of Miss Holling's telling us that Baynes was afraid of her."

"I have added it to the list of the many things I do not yet know about this case."

"It seems to me that it keeps on getting more complicated."

"Precisely."

Holmes ate his supper in silence and then retreated to his armchair and his pipe. From time to time, he stood up and paced back and forth the length of the room. I knew enough not to interrupt him, and at ten o'clock, when I headed up to my bedroom, he was still smoking and pacing.

Chapter Twenty-Seven

It was the Season of Darkness

"**W**ATSON, WAKE UP!" Holmes shouted to me from the door of my room.

"Merciful heavens, this is the third night in a row. What is it this time?"

"We have a visitor, and she needs your attention. Do hurry."

"What time is it?"

"Nearly five o'clock. No more questions. Kindly make haste."

I pulled on my dressing gown and staggered down the stairs. Sitting on the sofa, dressed in her nightclothes and dressing gown, was Miss Linda Holling, and she was holding her left arm tightly with her right hand.

"For goodness' sake," she said. "It's just a cut. I'm not dying."

"Let me have a look at it," I said. She pulled her hand away and exposed a rather nasty cut on her upper arm. It had bled significantly, but the pressure she had applied to it had staunched the flow of blood. No arteries or veins had been touched, and a bit of antiseptic and a tight bandage would suffice.

"What happened?"

"It could have been much worse," she said. "I escaped in time."

"Good Lord, from what?"

"No Watson," said Holmes. "From *whom?* Before she gives her full account, might I impose on your good graces to fetch her a cup of tea?"

"And a bit of brandy," she added, "if you don't mind."

After half-a-cup of generously adulterated tea, Miss Holling's color had returned, and she appeared to be quite composed. Holmes had, uncharacteristically, waited patiently and now requested that she give us a complete account.

"I have two cats," she said and took another swallow of her tea.

"That's nice to know, madam," said Holmes. "Are they pertinent to your account?"

"Very. I would not be here had it not been for them. An hour ago, I was awakened by Charles Darnay, he's the large grey one, when he started screeching. The other, Sidney Carton, joined him and started up as well."

"Miss Holling," I said, "forgive my interrupting you, but why would you call your cats by those names?"

"Because they are the best of Toms and the worst of Toms. And tonight, they proved to be the best."

Inwardly, I swore that I would never understand the minds of women who owned cats, but I said nothing, and Miss Holling carried on.

"They never make a row like that, and I knew that something must be wrong. I listened, and I was sure I heard someone moving around downstairs. I thought at first it was someone trying to rob me. Now, I admit that I was quite frightened, but I do not own anything of any value, and I assumed that whoever it was would see that straight away and leave. But then I heard him coming up the stairs."

"Goodness gracious," I said, "did you shout for the police?"

"No, Doctor. St. John's Wood is a very respectable neighborhood. Our policemen walk past my house every two hours on the quarter-hour. One had passed by quite recently, and it would be almost two hours before he came back."

"Do you keep a weapon in your bedroom?" I asked.

"I used to when I went overseas for the Royal Navy, but not in West London. No, I thought I was safe here. All I could do was push the dresser in front of the door and hope that would keep him out. He opened the door and started to push against the dresser, and it was moving backward, so I went for the window, but it was stuck. So, I picked up the small chair I have by my bed, and I smashed it through the window, and I climbed out and that's how I cut my arm. And then I got on my bicycle and came here."

"Why," said Holmes, "did you come here instead of finding a policeman?"

"That should be obvious, Mr. Holmes. I have no enemies in the world. Whoever came to attack me must be connected in some way to what has happened in the Vanderstone family, and it could only be as a result of our conversation this afternoon. I think that to be irrefutably logical. Don't you?"

"Yes, that does seem to be the only reasonable conclusion."

"Well then, you had best get moving on it. I have a mountain of work still to do to sort out the mess I was left with and would like to get back to it by nine. Now then, it is not safe for me to return home, so if you do not mind fetching me a blanket and pillow, I shall spend the remainder of the night here on your sofa."

I felt a surge of panic as I recalled what happened to the last woman who slept on our sofa.

"Please assure me," I said, "that you have not brought any bottles of medicine with you."

"I brought nothing but my slippers and clothes. However, you can leave your bottle of brandy on the coffee table."

At half past seven the next morning, the holiday Monday of the Bank Holiday weekend, Miss Holling, Holmes and I hailed a cab and had the driver take us to St. John's Wood.

"You wait in the cab, please, Miss Holling," I said. "We will enter your home and make certain that no one is waiting for you."

I had my service revolver out and at the ready. Holmes had slipped a small Webley Bulldog into his pocket and brought his Penang Lawyer rather than his customary walking stick. I approached the front door and tried the handle. It opened. We slowly entered and searched the entire lower floor. There was no one there except for the two of us, and nothing appeared to have been disturbed.

I jumped in fear when I heard a loud screech and then relaxed, realizing that a cat had objected to my presence.

"Easy there, Sidney," I said. "And stay away from guillotines."

I made my way up the stairs with Holmes behind me. Again, we encountered no one except the second cat. The only indication of anyone having been there recently was the out-of-place dresser in Miss Holling's bedroom and the broken window. As she had smashed from the inside, most of the slivers of glass had been blasted to the outside, with only a very few on the floor in the bedroom.

Once we were convinced that there was no assailant waiting for her, I hurried back out to the cab and informed her that it was safe to re-enter.

"Please check," said Holmes, "and tell me if anything has been taken."

She ignored the cats who were demanding their breakfast and glanced around the parlor and the kitchen before proceeding upstairs.

"I'll have to fix the window," she said, "but that's all. Perhaps I should put a lock on the bedroom door. But otherwise ... oh, oh..."

"What is it?" said Holmes.

Miss Holling was standing in the doorway of her closet and looking at the interior.

"The file box. They found the locked cabinet and forced it open. The file box is gone."

Chapter Twenty-Eight

Dogs and Children

"**K**indly tell me," said Holmes, "who, other than you and Lady Giselle, knew of the existence and location of the box?"

"Only you and Doctor Watson. I told you about it yesterday."

"I assure you, madam, it was neither me nor the doctor who violated your privacy last night. Did Lady Giselle come personally each time she wished to hide her papers? Did she ever send one of her minions?"

"Never. She did not even hand them to me. It was only ever her."

"Very well, then. At some time in the recent past, someone must have followed her and observed her actions. Did anyone ever accompany her in a cab or carriage perhaps?"

"Not that I observed. Of course, one cannot see into the interior of a carriage, so that is possible. But no one ever entered my house except her."

"How very interesting. Thank you, madam. It is now morning, and your neighborhood has come alive. Do you feel safe if we leave you here on your own?"

"I have a service revolver locked away in the cellar. I could bring it out and load it, if necessary. My two tomcats serve as useful sentries. I shall be quite all right."

"Splendid. I doubt anyone will return, as whoever it was appears to have found what he was after. But if they return, do not hesitate to shoot them, preferably in the leg so that they can still be arrested whilst alive."

We left the very capable lady and departed.

"If you don't mind, Watson, I should like to return home through the Park. I need time to consider all of the data we have now received. Kindly accompany me, but do not say anything unless I ask something of you."

He had started walking toward Regent's Park before I had time to respond.

We walked south on Avenue Road and entered the park at the northwest corner. We had not gone more than a few yards before Holmes stopped, looked ahead and muttered something that I have chosen not to record. It being a glorious sunny morning on a holiday Monday, the park was teeming with families and young children, all flying kites and playing games. The flat open pitches were full of young men kicking a football around. The sky was dappled with fluttering kites, and dogs were barking incessantly. Holmes's plans for a contemplative walk were dashed by waves of happy Londoners.

"Come now, my friend," I said. "You spent the entire weekend with a horrible family. May as well cheer up when you are surrounded by respectable ones."

"My dear Watson, it was a wise fellow who once said that any man who hates dogs and children cannot be all bad. But come, there is a bench in the wooded area beside the Boating Lake that is far from the madding crowd."

He walked quickly to his chosen destination, sat down and gazed into the trees. It was clear to me that we were not going to

151

move for some time, so I took out my notebook and scribbled several pages of tentative lines. A distant clock had just chimed the eleventh hour when I heard him whisper, "Yes … yes … of course … that's it."

He leapt to his feet and brought his hands together in a single resounding clap.

"What? What is it?" I said.

His face had for a moment assumed a look I had come to know well over the past two decades. His eyes had that peculiar gleam to them. The lion about to pounce had returned. Then the look vanished.

"Confound it!" he shouted.

"What? What now?"

"It's a holiday."

"That news makes most of us happy, Holmes. What is wrong?"

"What is wrong is that I have work to do and most offices are closed. Well, never mind. I'll have to attend to everything on Tuesday. Please be prepared to accompany me back to their house on Wednesday morning. Until then, do enjoy your holiday."

He turned and marched, indeed nearly jogged, off in the direction of Marylebone, leaving me alone on a bench in the middle of a copse of trees.

Chapter Twenty-Nine

Please Take Notes

Every doctor's surgery in England is busy on the day after a holiday weekend. Mine kept me going from dawn to dark with all those dear English folk who struggle to stay healthy on the weekend and need an excuse for their lethargy on the morning after. A good thing it was too, for me. Otherwise, I would have been on needles and pins, wondering what in the world Holmes was up to. He had vanished, and I did not see him until six o'clock on the morning of Wednesday, 27 August 1902.

I had set my alarm, not wanting to be late for whatever he had planned. I hurried to prepare myself for the day, and when I bounced down the stairs to our front room, he was already sitting at our breakfast table.

"Eat up, my friend," he said. "We have a full day ahead. Lestrade should be along any minute now."

Thankfully, Mrs. Hudson had returned, and I wolfed down the fine full English she had dutifully organized for us and was in the process of gulping down my last mouthful of coffee when the bell rang at our Baker Street door. A minute later, I heard a man— Inspector Lestrade, I assumed—ascending the stairs. He was no longer a young man, but the pace of his steps was surprisingly vigorous. He too must have anticipated some ecstatic event about to envelope us.

"You better be right this time, Holmes," said Lestrade as he entered the room.

"I showed you the evidence last evening, my dear Inspector, and here you are. I must assume that this time, I have hit the target."

"What evidence?" I said.

"My dear Watson, the Inspector and I thought it best by far that we not reveal it to you—"

"I beg your pardon! Now look here, Holmes, if after all these years, you cannot—"

"Cannot have faith in your ability to remain completely objective? You are entirely correct, my friend. You are utterly too supportive and trusting of me to fail to see where I might have made a failure in judgment. We need you to be a completely disinterested observer. You must be present this morning with not a hint of any pre-conceived notions about what you will see take place. It is one of the most significant requests I have ever made of you. Would you not agree with me, Inspector?"

"Right. You'll have to be watching the lot of them and observing. It's terribly important. Right."

"Oh, well, fine," I muttered. "If that is the way it has to be, well, then, carry on, I suppose."

"Splendid," said Holmes. "But do bring your service revolver with you. One never knows. Now, we have to be up at Primrose Hill before our dear friends go to their important senior positions in the City and their wives head off to the offices of their charity."

Lestrade's carriage was waiting on Baker Street to take us, and a larger police carriage filled with constables followed along. We rolled up the drive of the Vanderstone's London house at half-past eight. Miss Holling arrived on her bicycle at the same time.

"I am terribly sorry, madam," Holmes said to her, "but I must again request that you return to your home and not be present here for at least the next hour. But please be assured that the evidence you provided was critical to the success of this investigation. I promise to come by your home later this morning and explain everything. But before you go, would you be so kind as to unlock the front door for us yet again?"

She did not look at all pleased but opened the door. Then one of the constables gallantly volunteered to accompany her home and push her bicycle back to her house. He was one of Lestrade's senior men, and I overheard him suggest that a stop for coffee on the High Street might be in order. I caught a glimpse of a smile on her face as they departed.

"Once more unto the breach, gentlemen," said Holmes, waving us all inside. "Please bring the occupants into the dining room and have them be seated."

The constables disappeared up the stairs, and within five minutes, Mr. and Mrs. Vanderstone and Mr. and Mrs. Baynes were seated at the table. All four were fashionably dressed and ready to spend their day in the heart of London. All four were looking daggers at us.

Holmes took me aside.

"My dear Watson, I have forgotten one detail. We need you to be entirely concentrated on observing their reactions. But that leaves no one to record what is said during the meeting. That was terribly negligent of me."

"I could try to do both tasks," I said.

"Oh, no, no. That won't do. Is there anyone else we could bring in to take down the notes?"

"Miss Holling could have, but you sent her home."

"Oh dear, how mindless of me. Is there no one else?"

"One of the constables?"

"Oh, goodness no. They are entirely conflicted. Lestrade is their superior, and they would never think to record anything he did that made him look as if he were in his dotage."

"That only leaves the new maid and the groom, and I doubt the girl can spell her name, let alone take a record of what is said. Shall I drag Othniel Clarke in here? He may be just a private, but he has a decent head on his shoulders."

"Ah, an excellent suggestion. Not as good as Miss Holling would have been, but he'll have to do. Would you mind running back to the stables and hauling him in?"

"Good morning, soldier!" I shouted as I exited the back door of the house. I did not have to go looking for him. He was standing outside the stables with the three horses we had ridden two days ago, all saddled up and ready to be mounted.

"Are you going for a ride?" I asked him.

"Oh, good morning, Doctor. No, not me. Umm ... but sometimes the wives like to go riding in the morning, and I have to have their horses ready. Is there something I can do for you? I'm a bit busy getting ready for them."

"Sherlock Holmes has requested to have you sit in on the meeting he and Scotland Yard are about to hold with the two couples. He wants you to record the conversations. I don't expect it to take long. You can just leave the horses. They'll be fine."

He took a quick look at his watch. "I ... I really can't. If the wives come out, they get cross if they have to wait. I'll have to finish getting their rides ready."

"Not a problem. The wives will be present at the meeting, so they will not be coming for a ride before it's over. Come, now. Here. I have your notepad and pencil ready for you. All that work you've been doing to better yourself is about to pay off. You are the official recording secretary of the meeting."

He offered a few more objections, but I would not hear of them. I took him firmly by the elbow and led him into the dining room. Everyone was looking at him, and the poor fellow was obviously embarrassed. He slunk into a chair in the corner of the room, took the pencil and pad in hand and kept his eyes on the floor.

"Ah, welcome, Mr. Clarke," said Holmes. "Excellent. Now we can get started."

Chapter Thirty

You Traitor

"**G**et started indeed! Now look here," said Bentley Baynes "enough is enough. We are on our way to situations, and your postponing us for no good reason is completely unacceptable. The constant presence of police officers is damaging the respected reputation of this home in the community. So, for whatever reason you are here yet again, get it over with and get out of here!"

"Something new and of interest has come up," said Holmes, "and we are obliged to share it with you."

"Well then, share it and be gone," said Baynes.

"It's about Lady Giselle. We had concluded that the four of you, and not without reason, despised and hated her. That conclusion is not in doubt. Where we erred was in not realizing that you put up with her because she was brilliant and was making all of you very rich. She and her father were the brains, as they say, of the enterprise. You four just did as you were told and watched your wealth increase."

"Nonsense," said Baynes. "My brother-in-law and I did no more than arrange the financing she and Lord Vanderstone required. That was our job irrespective of Giselle. And what we did was entirely legal. Our wives had no role in these matters whatsoever. You made misleading accusations on this matter yesterday, and they were shown to be false and dismissed. You are wasting our time. Now, if you have something useful to say, then say it or go home, Mr. Holmes."

"Ah, but yesterday, I did not know that Lady Giselle kept complete records of all the transactions you carried out and the correspondence back and forth between the four of you and herself."

Holmes paused here. An apprehensive silence had descended on the room.

"For example, she may have made references to the fine charity work carried out by Mrs. Baynes and Mrs. Vanderstone. Your charity, ladies, is the Society for Universal Aid, is it not?"

"It is," said Mrs. Baynes. "That is public knowledge. You have *discovered* nothing."

Mrs. Vanderstone sneezed and wiped her nose.

"Nothing? Perhaps the shipping of bales of used clothing to poor people in Africa, Asia and South America who are regarded as enemies of the British Empire is nothing to you, madam. I suspect that Department of War might have a different opinion."

"All our shipments were sent and delivered to destitute woman and children. *We* have no enemies under the age of twelve, Mr. Holmes, regardless of whether or not you do. Yet again, you have unearthed not a single piece of evidence against us."

"Not exactly true, I am sorry to say. You see, I did discover a box of letters and files kept by Lady Estelle in what was supposed to be a secret location."

Holmes paused again and glanced around the room. In my role as observer, I scrutinized the faces of the four of them. Whether it was on the battlefield or in a hospital, I had learned to know fear when I saw it in someone's eyes. I was looking at it.

"Unbeknownst to any of you, apparently, Lady Giselle recently moved the location of her file box to a locked compartment in the home of Miss Linda Holling. It was so much more convenient for her there than at its previous location. On the night before last, that compartment was opened by force and the contents removed and read. It has been revealed that all of you, along with Lord Vanderstone and Giselle, engaged for several years in shipping millions of pounds worth of small arms and light artillery all over the world."

"Of course, we did," said Bentley, "and proud we are of it. Every single rifle and cartridge went to regiments of the BEF."

"No, sir, they did not. You and your step-father before you sold to anyone who had the money to pay you, starting with the Afghans twenty years ago. In the recent past, you have supplied the Boers, the natives in North Borneo, the Aro people in Nigeria, the Boxers in China, the Mahdis in the Sudan, and the Puntis in Hong Kong. All of these were enemies of Great Britain at the time you sent arms to them, hidden inside the bales of used clothing so charitably sent to the poor mothers and children."

Baynes rose to his feet and smacked his fist on the table. "And all of them struggling for their freedom—"

"SHUT YOUR MOUTH!" Mrs. Baynes screamed at her husband. She now stood up and announced, "No one will say anything more to the police or Sherlock Holmes. Constance, go now and place a phone call to our barristers and solicitors, and tell them to come here immediately."

"I'm ... I'm sorry," said Mrs. Vanderstone. "I've forgotten their names."

"Bickers and Slaughter. Their office is in Chancery Lane. Now go. Now!"

She turned to Holmes and Lestrade. "This meeting is over until our legal counsel arrives. You will leave our premises straight away. You may return after we meet with our lawyers."

"Well now," said Inspector Lestrade, "I am sorry to have to contradict you, but I'm afraid it will be you four who are leaving the premises. Based on the evidence I have received, I am charging the four of you with treason."

Lestrade then enunciated the charge and gave the required caution. Two of his constables stepped forward and politely asked the Vanderstones and the Bayneses to follow them out to the waiting police carriage. Bentley Baynes started several times to argue, but each time was ordered into silence by his wife. The other constables followed them, leaving Lestrade, Holmes, me, and Othniel Clarke alone in the room.

As soon as the others had gone, Holmes strode over to the corner where Clarke was seated. He reached down and snatched the pad on which he had been taking notes.

"Thank you, my good man. Now, if you would not mind waiting for me out by the stables, I have some good news for you."

The young soldier looked thoroughly confused but stood up and stepped over beside me.

"What's he going to do?" he whispered.

"I have no idea. Please just wait out by the stables. I'll be there to join you when he comes out."

Clarke walked out of the room, and I approached Holmes.

"You found the file box? Where?"

"I didn't find it. Not yet."

"But you said—"

"I said it had been found and its contents read. And most assuredly that happened. I did not say I had done it. I deduced the probable nature of the contents and, going by their reaction, was correct. Now then, we need to have a pleasant chat with Private Clarke."

Chapter Thirty-One

He's Getting Away

I started to head out of the house and to the stables, but Holmes pulled Lestrade aside and handed him the notes Othniel Clarke had written. He pointed to something on one of the pages, and Lestrade formed his lips into a duckbill and nodded. I waited for the two of them to catch up and was about to inquire concerning whatever it was that Clarke had written when Holmes breezed past me and called out to the young soldier.

"A word, if I may? And do relax. It may be good news."

"Certainly, Mr. Holmes. I'm a bit busy with the horses, but I never mind any bit of good news I get these days." He took a glance at his watch and looked back at Holmes.

"It is about what took place in the war," said Holmes. "Over the past two days, I have been doing extensive research concerning this family and, inevitably, it included the tragic death of Captain Vanderstone. There are some unanswered questions, it seems, about the incident that took his life."

"I thought you said it was good news. There's nothing good about that."

His short-lived smile had vanished, and he looked awfully low.

"Really, Holmes," I said. "You have already taken him through that horrible event. Do you have to do it again?"

"I do indeed. You see, Mr. Clarke, there is a possibility not only that your captain could be exonerated, but also that he could be posthumously awarded both the Queen's South Africa Medal and maybe the King's South Africa Medal as well."

That brought an outright grin to the scarred face.

"You don't say. Why, that would be a spot of all right. What is it you're needing to know from me?"

"To begin with, did Captain Vanderstone serve beyond the first of January of this current year."

"No, it was at the Battle of Tugela Heights that we were ambushed. That was before the turn of the New Year."

"Oh dear, I was afraid of that. That puts the King's Medal out of reach. It is only available to those who had lasted at least eighteen months, and their time there crossed over in 1902. But never mind. He is eligible for the Queen's Medal if we can straighten out the account of what happened."

"I've already told you all I can remember, sir." He took another quick look at his watch.

"Yes, you did. But there are some discrepancies. From what I read in one of the accounts on file, it was reported that Captain Vanderstone was not present when the attack started, but when the shell landed on the building where his men were staying, he rushed back into the flames and attempted to save his men. Did you see him do that, Clayton? And when he was there, another shell hit, and he lost his life. That makes him out to be a hero, if you ask me, even if his judgment in choosing the site for their bivouac was faulty. Can you confirm any of that?"

"Not for certain, sir. As I told you before, I had gone to the latrine and was just coming back when the shell hit and knocked me into next week. But I can tell you for sure that he was a good and brave soldier and did what he did for the love of his country."

"Excellent. Now, someone who was not very well disposed to Captain Vanderstone reported that he was trading with some local merchants for gold and diamonds. Did you ever witness any of that?"

When he glanced yet again at his watch, I interrupted.

"Private Clarke, are we keeping you from something?"

"No, Doctor. Well, in a way, sir. There's a party coming by any time now to look at buying one or two of our horses. Lady Giselle told me to sell them off, and I sent out a note to some folks I thought might be interested, and they should be here right soon. Would it be all right, Mr. Holmes, if'n we continued this talk a bit later today?"

He had no soon finished speaking than three people came around the corner of the house and were approaching the stables. There were two men and one woman, and they were all dressed in fashionable riding clothes.

Othniel started to walk, indeed to run, toward them. "Please wait inside, Mr. Holmes," he shouted back over his shoulder. "I won't be long."

I was about to head back into the house when I caught a good look at the older of the two men. I knew him. He was a small, alert person, very neat and dapper, in a perfectly tailored riding jacket and breeches, with trim little side-whiskers and an eye-glass.

"Colonel Ross!" I shouted to him. He looked at me and then at Holmes and shouted back.

"Good Lord. Sherlock Holmes and Dr. Watson. What in the blazes are you two doing here?"

"The blazes indeed," I said as I walked toward him. "How is dear old Silver Blaze?"

Neither Holmes nor I had seen Colonel Ross, the owner of King's Pyland in Dartmoor, since the running of the Wessex Cup over a decade ago, but other than the inescapable ravages of age, he still looked the elegant, well-known sportsman.

"My dear Colonel," said Holmes, approaching him with an outstretched hand. "What brings you all the way from Wessex to the suburbs of London?"

Othniel Clarke stepped up until he was almost between Holmes and the Colonel.

"He's just here on some horse business, Mr. Holmes. If you and the Doctor wait inside, I'm sure the cooks will have something for you whilst we get the business over with, and then you can all catch up and have a friendly chat."

"Young man," said Colonel Ross, "I am in no hurry, and I am still under obligation to Sherlock Holmes for the great service he did for me. For a city bloke, he has a wonderful eye for a good horse. So, join us, Holmes, whilst we look at this horse of old Lord Vanderstone's. Oh, and this is my daughter, Lilly, and you must remember Silas Brown, even if he now not quite as spry as he used to be."

We exchanged greetings, and Holmes gestured toward the three horses with saddle and bridle and waiting to be ridden, it now appeared, by the three visitors.

"Are you going to buy a horse, Colonel?"

"Oh, no. I have a fine mare that is about to be in estrus, and we only want to borrow Starless Midnight to look after her. But I always like to get up on any stallion I'm paying for stud work and assure myself that he is up to snuff. Four hundred pounds does not grow on trees, you know."

"I do know," said Holmes, "and I also know that you will not be able to ride Starless Midnight today or any day."

"Why not?"

"Because he is not here."

"He most surely is. I'm looking at him. That black horse over there is the one that won the Grand National."

Holmes turned and looked at the black stallion. "What horse? I do not see the horse you are talking about."

"Mr. Holmes, I am not blind. Now, are you making a bad joke, or are you insulting me?"

"I am saving you four hundred pounds. You were about to be swindled by this young man, who has continued the fraud perpetrated by Lord Vanderstone."

He then turned to Othniel Clarke. "I see why you were in a hurry to get rid of us. You are taking four hundred pounds a week in stud fees but only depositing two hundred into the estate account."

The groom was blushing terribly, and his scarred face looked utterly freakish with the mix of glowing red and white scar tissue.

"Lady Giselle," he said, "she had me do it. It was her what set everything for us. She was the one who contracted with the Colonel, and the two hundred pounds was what I got to keep. It was all her."

"Was it now?" said Holmes. "But you have continued the fraud and have reapplied the black dye to the white patches of *Feet of Silver,* haven't you, Clayton? And not only that, you have applied it to your hair. You should have never let me get so close to you that I could see your blond roots. And twice now, you have not noticed when I called you by your true name, Captain Clayton Vanderstone!"

Utter panic had spread across his face, and he was sputtering in an attempt to speak.

"Fine. I am. But there's no felony crime in trying to hide my shame. I didn't take anything that did not belong to me."

"No, but when you learned from your sister that your father had been sending arms to the Boers, the very people who killed your men and burnt your face to a crisp, you were consumed with anger at him. Your own father had supplied the arms that brought about your disaster. You took your revenge … and you killed him!"

"NO! You cannot prove that!"

"All the proof I need is sitting in Giselle's file box, and we are about to find it inside the stables."

He looked as if he was about to run, but in an instant, the firm hands of Inspector Lestrade and myself were on his arms. holding him back. I was in shock and could not believe what I was hearing from Holmes.

Holmes continued. "You attached yourself to your sister. She was the only one who knew your secret. But she was too clever for her own good. You knew it was only a matter of time until she figured out what you had done. She trusted you, but she worshipped her father. You knew that she would expose you and have you arrested, and you got rid of her, didn't you? And the maid saw something, so you chatted her up, gave her cupboard love like you do the cooks, drugged her, and killed her too."

"It … it … it was self-defense," he screamed. "She … she would have killed me like she killed our stepmother. I knew she did that. I was only defending myself."

"Tell that to the jury," said Holmes.

Lestrade had let go of him and was holding a pair of handcuffs. Then the man I knew and had cared about as Othniel Clark twisted violently and broke free from me. He was off like a rocket, his limp vanished, and he ran directly toward the black stallion. In a move practiced by cowboys in the American West, he raced at the rear end of the horse, placed his hands on the haunches and vaulted into the saddle. The horse reared up and then, feeling a hard set of heels kicking into his flanks, took off at a gallop toward the parkland.

"He's getting away!" said Lestrade, announcing the obvious. "He can gallop clear from here to Marylebone Station. If he makes it there, we'll have lost him."

"Then we had better give chase," said Holmes as he put his foot in the stirrup of the same chestnut thoroughbred we had ridden on Saturday. "Care to join me, Inspector?"

"Not on your life, Holmes," said Lestrade. "I know my limits, and steeplechase riding is well beyond them. Take these darbies and bring him in if you catch him."

Holmes grabbed the handcuffs and turned to me.

"Watson! Up you get! The chase is afoot."

For a passing instant, I thought his choice of metaphor inappropriate, but I mounted the dun mare and grabbed the reins.

"We'll never catch him," I said.

"I do believe we shall," said Holmes, and he kicked his horse into a gallop. I did likewise, and soon we were moving at breakneck speed across the open grasslands of Primrose Hill. I was convinced it was a fool's errand and that by now the stallion would be almost down the hill and ready to cross over into The Regent's Park.

After a minute of hard riding, we turned the corner and entered the stretch that would lead us to the stone wall where Holmes had nearly killed himself on Saturday.

To my complete surprise, I could see Clayton Vanderstone on *Feet of Silver,* and he was trotting back in our direction. When he was a hundred or so feet on our side of the wall, he turned the stallion around and galloped him directly at the wall. The horse ran at full speed and then reared and stopped.

"He won't jump the wall!" I shouted at Holmes. "You spooked him. He remembers."

In another minute, we had caught up to Clayton Vanderstone, and I came up beside him with my service revolver drawn.

"Down you get, soldier."

Chapter Thirty-Two

Out With It, Holmes

At one o'clock, Holmes, Lestrade, Miss Holling and I gathered around a lunch table at the Duke of York pub. A lovely young barmaid named Angel greeted us by name and waited on us.

"Would you like me to keep that thing at the bar whilst you enjoy your meal?" she asked us, pointing to the file box in the middle of the table.

"No, my dear," I said. "It's our table center. We quite enjoy looking at it."

She gave me a sideways look, smiled sweetly and laid out our lunch.

"All right, Holmes," said Lestrade, "out with it. How did you know?"

"First things first, Inspector. I must apologize to both Miss Holling and to my dearest friend. Madam, it might have been quite useful to have had you participate in our meeting this morning, but I feared you might not be able to keep a straight face when I pretended that we had found and read the contents of this file box. And you, my dear Doctor, are terribly inept at deceiving people. You are much too honest a man. I needed you to be unaware of the evidence I had gathered concerning Clayton Vanderstone so that you could convince him to be present at the meeting without suspecting anything. Yet again, I am in your debt for the fine job you did."

"Well, fine, you're welcome. So glad I could be such a useful dupe."

"You were splendid. Now, as to the evidence. Inspector Lestrade will confirm that there is seldom one piece of it that gives away the case. It is cumulative. One item after another is observed until a hypothesis is reached. We began with Lady Giselle herself. You were there, Watson. Tell me, are you hard of hearing?"

That question struck me as a bit of an insult.

"I beg your pardon!?" I said and then realized that my question was precisely the wrong way to respond to his. "No, I am not."

"And neither am I. Nor was multi-lingual Lady Giselle in the habit of mumbling her words. She quite distinctly said *brother,* not *brother's.*" He exaggerated the *zzzz* sound at the end of the word.

"After our little riding excursion and my being thrown from my horse, I noticed the black dye on my hand. The explanation the groom gave was plausible except that the dye was fresh. Had the fraudulent stud service been terminated by Lady Giselle, that dye would have completely dried and started to wear off. They were continuing to swindle racehorse owners."

"I do feel badly," I said, "for Colonel Ross. He came all the way from Dartmoor for no good reason."

"Oh, don't worry about him," said Miss Holling. "I had a lovely chat with him when you brought me back to the house. I offered to sell him all three horses, and he accepted."

"Brilliant," said Holmes. "Until further notice, it appears, madam, you are still needed to manage the estate. But back to our devious groom. Twice he lied to us, indicating he was not an entirely honest young man. He eavesdropped and must have done so again from the open window whilst we were meeting with Miss Holling, and he heard about the hidden file box. Everyone else in the house was out on the lawn playing their croquet game. To that was added Dr. Watson's very thorough report of his long chat with him."

"What about that?" I asked. "It was a perfectly civil conversation."

"No doubt, and I do not wish to be seen as having a prejudice against privates who have taken the King's shilling and served bravely in His Majesty's army, but they are not known for debating military strategy, nor reading the classics, nor understanding Latin. Then there was the photo of Clayton and Giselle with their father. The boy in the picture had blond hair, like his sister. As I am sure any woman who dyes her hair can tell you, only a few days are needed for the roots and true color to creep in. I observed them on the first day we met as I looked down on him from my horse. The following day, they had vanished."

"Go on, Holmes," said Lestrade as he tucked into his plate of fish and chips and mushy peas. "What else?"

"The feed order for the horses."

"The what?" said Lestrade.

"There were only four horses in the London stables. An average horse needs fifteen to twenty pounds of hay a day. A vigorous thoroughbred may require twenty-five. A standing order of seven hundred pounds of hay was far in excess of what was needed for four horses. The only explanation is that the stables were also being used for additional horses—mares approaching estrus and waiting to be serviced by the stallion at a cost of three or four hundred pounds a round. Again, it was probable evidence that the fraud was continuing."

Holmes stopped, took a long sip on his ale, and then leaned back in his chair.

"Of course, the *pièce de resistance was watching Clayton as he took notes. Inspector Lestrade was in charge of that. What did you observe, Inspector?"*

"Right, well, he took them capably and quickly up to the time you told everyone about the file box. I thought he was going to drop

non italics

171

his bloody jaw on the floor. The look on his face was laughable, but I dared not laugh, or that would have given away the game. It was proof enough for me that he must have been the one who broke into Miss Holling's home and stole it. You could see on his notepad where his pencil spasmed right across the page."

"And where," said Miss Holling, "if you don't mind my asking, did you find the file box?"

"Under some hay bales in the stables," said Holmes, "which was exactly where the inspector and I guessed we might find it. Our examination of the contents so far has been cursory, but it appears that Lady Giselle kept enough information to convict the family of treason and, we expect, her brother of murder."

"It would have convicted your client too," said Lestrade. "Lucky for you, she is no longer around."

"An odd view of luck, I must say. However, we now have the lot of them."

"The murder charge against the groom may be hard to prove," said Lestrade.

"I agree," said Holmes, "but the charge of fraud in his swindling of the racehorse owners will stick. As most of our judges are drawn from the noble class and either own horses themselves or are part of the set who do, we can count on them to deliver a stiff penalty of years in prison to anyone who had the temerity to hoodwink one of their ilk."

We all paused at this point and enjoyed a few more mouthfuls of our lunch. I reflected on the events of the morning and turned to Holmes.

"Let me try to understand all this," I said. "You are telling us that Clayton Vanderstone was away from his men and dealing with gold and diamond merchants when they were ambushed."

"Correct," said Holmes. "He was not without courage and exceptional loyalty to the Empire. He did indeed rush back onto the conflagration to try to save his men. He failed and ended up terribly burned himself. But knowing his guilt would be exposed, and even

172

NON ITALIC

though badly injured, he had the presence of mind to dress himself in the uniform of one of his fallen men and take on a false identity. He had been gone from the household for almost a decade whilst he attended university and tried his hand at acting, and it is not surprising that with his hair dyed and his face scarred, his step-siblings did not know who he truly was. It is possible that his father threatened to disown him. We shall never know. But his sister clearly knew who he was and, as all younger sisters are of their older brothers, she quite adored him and trusted him."

"But then," I said, "he found out about the treasonous shipments of arms and took his revenge and found a way to bring about the death of his father."

"Precisely. We do not know if she, out of loyalty to the father, then threatened to turn him in or if he took out his vengeance on her as well. But the only reasonable possibility is that it was he who poisoned the medicine after eavesdropping on the scheme attempted by Cuthbert Molesworth. I suspect that his devious spying had revealed Molesworth's game, or if he added poison to the bottle just to be sure it worked."

"You've completely discounted the quack doctor?" asked Lestrade.

"His claim that he is too greedy and too lazy to want to kill the goose that was about to lay his golden eggs is credible. Although I do hope that Dr. Watson will file a complaint with the General Medical Council and have him put out of business."

"Right," said Lestrade. "It looks like there will be justice done all around."

"What happens to the estate?" I asked, "It is worth well over a million pounds."

"No doubt," said Holmes, "had his plan worked, Clayton would have revealed his identity and tried to claim his inheritance. With him removed then, to the best of my knowledge, the next relative in line is the Bayneses' daughter, who, I believe, has just turned sixteen years of age."

"Merciful heavens," I said, "she is going to be one of the richest young women in all of England. How can she be expected to look after all that?"

"She will require a competent person to manage it all for her. Fortunately, the exact person she needs is sitting at this table."

Three sets of eyes turned to Miss Linda Holling.

"It would appear," she said, "that I will not be looking for a new position after all. I've met the daughter several times—Lillian is her name. She is beautiful, highly intelligent and much too much like her mother. I expect that she will be the most talked-about debutante of next year's season. She may be rich and gorgeous, but she will carry a frightful reputation with her mother in prison and a cluster of murders in her family."

"Perhaps," said Holmes. "Watson, the fair sex is your department. What do you think of her prospects?"

I thought for a minute and then sighed. "An Englishman hates to admit it, but we all know that if a young debutante is sufficiently attractive and also awfully rich, well, who needs a reputation?"

Dear Sherlockian Reader:

The genesis of this story was my reading of *The Last Slave Ships*, by John Harris. It recounted how the slave trade had continued long after it had been outlawed by the British Empire in 1807 and slavery itself in 1834. The illegal transport of slaves from Africa, using ships flagged with the American flag, continued until 1867. Slavery itself was practiced in Cuba and Brazil until the 1880s, two decades after the Emancipation and the Thirteenth Amendment.

Although it is not touched on in this story, slavery was not abolished in many countries until well into the twentieth century. The transport and trafficking of indentured laborers continue to this day. Unfortunately, we do not have a wonderful detective like Sherlock Holmes around to help put an end to it.

The presentation of debutantes was initiated in 1780 by King George III in honor of his wife, Queen Charlotte. Its original purpose was as a fundraiser for a couple of London hospitals. Each year, the daughters of noble families aged 16 to 19 would be presented as *debutantes*. After the Ball, the annual 'London Season' began in which the debutantes and eligible noble bachelors would attend a series of social events with the hope of being introduced to an appropriate potential marriage partner.

The tradition continued until the 1950s, when Queen Elizabeth put an end to it. It has been reported that Prince Philip considered the event 'bloody daft' and Princess Margaret complained that 'every tart in London is getting in.' Subsequent efforts to revive it had met with feeble results.

Primrose Hill is an open park area that abuts the northern border of The Regent's Park in London. The presence of manor houses with adjoining stables on the west side of it is fictitious. I made that one up. The locations named in Regent's Park are correct and are still there today.

The reference to *The Grapes* pub is accurate. It has been in operation for several hundred years and continues to this day in the same location. Dickens described it in the words quoted in the story. I have yet to pay a visit to it but will someday.

The game of Contract Bridge as it is played today was not codified or popularly embraced until the 1920s. Its forerunner, *Royal Auction Bridge,* is believed to have been invented by bored British soldiers serving under the Raj and was imported to Great Britain around the time this story is set. Croquet was imported from France and, for a while, was quite the rage in England. Its popularity was supplanted by lawn tennis.

The Second Boer War was fought in what is now South Africa from October 1899 until May 1902. Regardless of the heroic accounts written about it (including one by Arthur Conan Doyle) and the monuments to the soldiers and battles (including one in my hometown of Toronto), it was absolutely not the Empire's finest hour. The references to it in the story are more or less accurate.

The Queen's South Africa Medal was awarded to soldiers who served with distinction during the war. King Edward VII initiated The King's South Africa Medal for those who served during the first year of his reign.

The term 'quack' as a name for a phony doctor has nothing to do with ducks. It is the diminutive of 'quacksalver' and was borrowed from the Dutch, who first used it for medical charlatans.

Amyl nitrate was used during the Victorian era as a heart stimulant. It was replaced in the twentieth century by nitroglycerin. However, it continued to be available and was used as the first generation of a recreational drug that is better known as 'poppers.'

The Grand National steeplechase horserace was started in 1839 and continues to this day. You may recall that Elizabeth (Velvet) Taylor won it in 1944.

The novels found in Lady Giselle's room were all from that era, and all dealt with the theme of female empowerment and/or revenge. Many of them are still read today.

Lourenço Marques was the name of the capital of the Portuguese colony of Mozambique. A railway line connected it with Pretoria.

After Mozambique became independent in 1976, the city was renamed Maputo.

References to locations throughout London are, to the best of my knowledge, accurate for 1902.

If you enjoyed this story or if there are ways it could have been improved, please help the author and future readers by leaving a constructive review on the site from which you obtained the book. Thank you. Much appreciated,

CSC

About the Author

In May of 2014, the Sherlock Holmes Society of Canada – better known as The Bootmakers – announced a contest for a new Sherlock Holmes story. Although he had no experience writing fiction, the author submitted a short Sherlock Holmes mystery and was blessed to be declared one of the winners. Thus inspired, he has continued to write new Sherlock Holmes Mysteries since and is on a mission to write a new story as a tribute to each of the sixty stories in the original Canon. He currently writes from Buenos Aires, Toronto, the Okanagan, and Manhattan. Several readers of New Sherlock Holmes Mysteries have kindly sent him suggestions for future stories. You are welcome to do likewise at: craigstephencopland@gmail.com.

www.SherlockHolmesMystery.com

Super Collections A and B

49 New Sherlock Holmes Mysteries.

The perfect ebooks for readers who subscribe to Kindle Unlimited.

www.SherlockHolmesMystery.com

The Adventure of the Dying Detective

The Original Sherlock Holmes Story

Arthur Conan Doyle

The Adventure of the Dying Detective

Mrs. Hudson, the landlady of Sherlock Holmes, was a long-suffering woman. Not only was her first-floor flat invaded at all hours by throngs of singular and often undesirable characters but her remarkable lodger showed an eccentricity and irregularity in his life which must have sorely tried her patience. His incredible untidiness, his addiction to music at strange hours, his occasional revolver practice within doors, his weird and often malodorous scientific experiments, and the atmosphere of violence and danger which hung around him made him the very worst tenant in London. On the other hand, his payments were princely. I have no doubt that the house might have been purchased at the price which Holmes paid for his rooms during the years that I was with him.

The landlady stood in the deepest awe of him and never dared to interfere with him, however outrageous his proceedings might seem. She was fond of him, too, for he had a remarkable gentleness and courtesy in his dealings with women. He disliked and distrusted the sex, but he was always a chivalrous opponent. Knowing how genuine was her regard for him, I listened earnestly to her story when she came to my rooms in the second year of my married life and told me of the sad condition to which my poor friend was reduced.

"He's dying, Dr. Watson," said she. "For three days he has been sinking, and I doubt if he will last the day. He would not let me get a doctor. This morning when I saw his bones sticking out of his face and his great bright eyes looking at me I could stand no more of it. 'With your leave or without it, Mr. Holmes, I am going for a doctor this very hour,' said I. 'Let it be Watson, then,' said he. I wouldn't waste an hour in coming to him, sir, or you may not see him alive."

I was horrified for I had heard nothing of his illness. I need not say that I rushed for my coat and my hat. As we drove back I asked for the details.

"There is little I can tell you, sir. He has been working at a case down at Rotherhithe, in an alley near the river, and he has brought this illness back with him. He took to his bed on Wednesday afternoon and has never moved since. For these three days neither food nor drink has passed his lips."

"Good God! Why did you not call in a doctor?"

"He wouldn't have it, sir. You know how masterful he is. I didn't dare to disobey him. But he's not long for this world, as you'll see for yourself the moment that you set eyes on him."

He was indeed a deplorable spectacle. In the dim light of a foggy November day the sick room was a gloomy spot, but it was that gaunt, wasted face staring at me from the bed which sent a chill to my heart. His eyes had the brightness of fever, there was a hectic flush upon either cheek, and dark crusts clung to his lips; the thin hands upon the coverlet twitched incessantly, his voice was croaking and spasmodic. He lay listlessly as I entered the room, but the sight of me brought a gleam of recognition to his eyes.

"Well, Watson, we seem to have fallen upon evil days," said he in a feeble voice, but with something of his old carelessness of manner.

"My dear fellow!" I cried, approaching him.

"Stand back! Stand right back!" said he with the sharp imperiousness which I had associated only with moments of crisis. "If you approach me, Watson, I shall order you out of the house."

"But why?"

"Because it is my desire. Is that not enough?"

Yes, Mrs. Hudson was right. He was more masterful than ever. It was pitiful, however, to see his exhaustion.

"I only wished to help," I explained.

"Exactly! You will help best by doing what you are told."

"Certainly, Holmes."

He relaxed the austerity of his manner.

"You are not angry?" he asked, gasping for breath.

Poor devil, how could I be angry when I saw him lying in such a plight before me?

"It's for your own sake, Watson," he croaked.

"For MY sake?"

"I know what is the matter with me. It is a coolie disease from Sumatra--a thing that the Dutch know more about than we, though they have made little of it up to date. One thing only is certain. It is infallibly deadly, and it is horribly contagious."

He spoke now with a feverish energy, the long hands twitching and jerking as he motioned me away.

"Contagious by touch, Watson--that's it, by touch. Keep your distance and all is well."

"Good heavens, Holmes! Do you suppose that such a consideration weighs with me of an instant? It would not affect me in the case of a stranger. Do you imagine it would prevent me from doing my duty to so old a friend?"

Again I advanced, but he repulsed me with a look of furious anger.

"If you will stand there I will talk. If you do not you must leave the room."

I have so deep a respect for the extraordinary qualities of Holmes that I have always deferred to his wishes, even when I least understood them. But now all my professional instincts were aroused. Let him be my master elsewhere, I at least was his in a sick room.

"Holmes," said I, "you are not yourself. A sick man is but a child, and so I will treat you. Whether you like it or not, I will examine your symptoms and treat you for them."

He looked at me with venomous eyes.

"If I am to have a doctor whether I will or not, let me at least have someone in whom I have confidence," said he.

"Then you have none in me?"

"In your friendship, certainly. But facts are facts, Watson, and, after all, you are only a general practitioner with very limited experience and mediocre qualifications. It is painful to have to say these things, but you leave me no choice."

I was bitterly hurt.

"Such a remark is unworthy of you, Holmes. It shows me very clearly the state of your own nerves. But if you have no confidence in me I would not intrude my services. Let me bring Sir Jasper Meek or Penrose Fisher, or any of the best men in London. But someone you MUST have, and that is final. If you think that I am going to stand here and see you die without either helping you myself or bringing anyone else to help you, then you have mistaken your man."

"You mean well, Watson," said the sick man with something between a sob and a groan. "Shall I demonstrate your own ignorance? What do you know, pray, of Tapanuli fever? What do you know of the black Formosa corruption?"

"I have never heard of either."

"There are many problems of disease, many strange pathological possibilities, in the East, Watson." He paused after each sentence to collect his failing strength. "I have learned so much during some recent researches which have a medico-criminal aspect. It was in the course of them that I contracted this complaint. You can do nothing."

"Possibly not. But I happen to know that Dr. Ainstree, the greatest living authority upon tropical disease, is now in London. All remonstrance is useless, Holmes, I am going this instant to fetch him." I turned resolutely to the door.

Never have I had such a shock! In an instant, with a tiger-spring, the dying man had intercepted me. I heard the sharp snap of a twisted key. The next moment he had staggered back to his bed, exhausted and panting after his one tremendous outflame of energy.

"You won't take the key from me by force, Watson, I've got you, my friend. Here you are, and here you will stay until I will otherwise. But I'll humour you." (All this in little gasps, with terrible struggles for breath between.) "You've only my own good at heart. Of course I know that very well. You shall have your way, but give me time to get my strength. Not now, Watson, not now. It's four o'clock. At six you can go."

"This is insanity, Holmes."

"Only two hours, Watson. I promise you will go at six. Are you content to wait?"

"I seem to have no choice. '

"None in the world, Watson. Thank you, I need no help in arranging the clothes. You will please keep your distance. Now, Watson, there is one other condition that I would make. You will seek help, not from the man you mention, but from the one that I choose "

"By all means."

"The first three sensible words that you have uttered since you entered this room, Watson. You will find some books over there. I am somewhat exhausted; I wonder how a battery feels when it pours electricity into a non-conductor? At six, Watson, we resume our conversation."

But it was destined to be resumed long before that hour, and in circumstances which gave me a shock hardly second to that caused by his spring to the door. I had stood for some minutes looking at the silent figure in the bed. His face was almost covered by the clothes and he appeared to be asleep. Then, unable to settle down to reading, I walked slowly round the room, examining the pictures of celebrated criminals with which every wall was adorned. Finally, in my aimless perambulation, I came to the mantelpiece. A litter of pipes, tobacco-pouches, syringes, penknives, revolver-cartridges, and other debris was scattered over it. In the midst of these was a small black and white ivory box with a sliding lid. It was a neat little thing, and I had stretched out my hand to examine it more closely, when----

It was a dreadful cry that he gave--a yell which might have been heard down the street. My skin went cold and my hair bristled at that horrible scream. As I turned I caught a glimpse of a convulsed face and frantic eyes. I stood paralyzed, with the little box in my hand.

"Put it down! Down, this instant, Watson--this instant, I say!" His head sank back upon the pillow and he gave a deep sigh of relief as I replaced the box upon the mantelpiece. "I hate to have my things touched, Watson. You know that I hate it. You fidget me beyond endurance. You, a doctor--you are enough to drive a patient into an asylum. Sit down, man, and let me have my rest!"

The incident left a most unpleasant impression upon my mind. The violent and causeless excitement, followed by this brutality of speech, so far removed from his usual suavity, showed me how deep was the disorganization of his mind. Of all ruins, that of a noble mind is the most deplorable. I sat in silent dejection until the stipulated time had passed. He seemed to have been watching the clock as well as I, for it was hardly six before he began to talk with the same feverish animation as before.

"Now, Watson," said he. "Have you any change in your pocket?"

"Yes."

"Any silver?"

"A good deal."

"How many half-crowns?"

"I have five."

"Ah, too few! Too few! How very unfortunate, Watson! However, such as they are you can put them in your watchpocket. And all the rest of your money in your left trouser pocket. Thank you. It will balance you so much better like that."

This was raving insanity. He shuddered, and again made a sound between a cough and a sob.

"You will now light the gas, Watson, but you will be very careful that not for one instant shall it be more than half on. I implore you to be careful, Watson. Thank you, that is excellent. No, you need not draw the blind. Now you will have the kindness to place some letters and papers upon this table within my reach. Thank you. Now some of that litter from the mantelpiece. Excellent, Watson! There is a sugar-tongs there. Kindly raise that small ivory box with its assistance. Place it here among the papers. Good! You can now go and fetch Mr. Culverton Smith, of 13 Lower Burke Street."

To tell the truth, my desire to fetch a doctor had somewhat weakened, for poor Holmes was so obviously delirious that it seemed dangerous to leave him. However, he was as eager now to consult the person named as he had been obstinate in refusing.

"I never heard the name," said I.

"Possibly not, my good Watson. It may surprise you to know that the man upon earth who is best versed in this disease is not a medical man, but a planter. Mr. Culverton Smith is a well-known resident of Sumatra, now visiting

London. An outbreak of the disease upon his plantation, which was distant from medical aid, caused him to study it himself, with some rather far-reaching consequences. He is a very methodical person, and I did not desire you to start before six, because I was well aware that you would not find him in his study. If you could persuade him to come here and give us the benefit of his unique experience of this disease, the investigation of which has been his dearest hobby, I cannot doubt that he could help me."

I gave Holmes's remarks as a consecutive whole and will not attempt to indicate how they were interrupted by gaspings for breath and those clutchings of his hands which indicated the pain from which he was suffering. His appearance had changed for the worse during the few hours that I had been with him. Those hectic spots were more pronounced, the eyes shone more brightly out of darker hollows, and a cold sweat glimmered upon his brow. He still retained, however, the jaunty gallantry of his speech. To the last gasp he would always be the master.

"You will tell him exactly how you have left me," said he. "You will convey the very impression which is in your own mind--a dying man--a dying and delirious man. Indeed, I cannot think why the whole bed of the ocean is not one solid mass of oysters, so prolific the creatures seem. Ah, I am wandering! Strange how the brain controls the brain! What was I saying, Watson?"

"My directions for Mr. Culverton Smith."

"Ah, yes, I remember. My life depends upon it. Plead with him, Watson. There is no good feeling between us. His nephew, Watson--I had suspicions of foul play and I allowed him to see it. The boy died horribly. He has a grudge against me. You will soften him, Watson. Beg him, pray him, get him here by any means. He can save me--only he!"

"I will bring him in a cab, if I have to carry him down to it."

"You will do nothing of the sort. You will persuade him to come. And then you will return in front of him. Make any excuse so as not to come with him. Don't forget, Watson. You won't fail me. You never did fail me. No doubt there are natural enemies which limit the increase of the creatures. You and I, Watson, we have done our part. Shall the world, then, be overrun by oysters? No, no; horrible! You'll convey all that is in your mind."

I left him full of the image of this magnificent intellect babbling like a foolish child. He had handed me the key, and with a happy thought I took it with me lest he should lock himself in. Mrs. Hudson was waiting, trembling and weeping, in the passage. Behind me as I passed from the flat I heard Holmes's high, thin voice in some delirious chant. Below, as I stood whistling for a cab, a man came on me through the fog.

"How is Mr. Holmes, sir?" he asked.

It was an old acquaintance, Inspector Morton, of Scotland Yard, dressed in unofficial tweeds.

"He is very ill," I answered.

He looked at me in a most singular fashion. Had it not been too fiendish, I could have imagined that the gleam of the fanlight showed exultation in his face.

"I heard some rumour of it," said he.

The cab had driven up, and I left him.

Lower Burke Street proved to be a line of fine houses lying in the vague borderland between Notting Hill and Kensington. The particular one at which my cabman pulled up had an air of smug and demure respectability in its old-fashioned iron railings, its massive folding-door, and its shining brasswork. All was in keeping with a solemn butler who appeared framed in the pink radiance of a tinted electrical light behind him.

"Yes, Mr. Culverton Smith is in. Dr. Watson! Very good, sir, I will take up your card."

My humble name and title did not appear to impress Mr. Culverton Smith. Through the half-open door I heard a high, petulant, penetrating voice.

"Who is this person? What does he want? Dear me, Staples, how often have I said that I am not to be disturbed in my hours of study?"

There came a gentle flow of soothing explanation from the butler.

"Well, I won't see him, Staples. I can't have my work interrupted like this. I am not at home. Say so. Tell him to come in the morning if he really must see me."

Again the gentle murmur.

"Well, well, give him that message. He can come in the morning, or he can stay away. My work must not be hindered."

I thought of Holmes tossing upon his bed of sickness and counting the minutes, perhaps, until I could bring help to him. It was not a time to stand upon ceremony. His life depended upon my promptness. Before the apologetic butler had delivered his message I had pushed past him and was in the room.

With a shrill cry of anger a man rose from a reclining chair beside the fire. I saw a great yellow face, coarse-grained and greasy, with heavy, double-chin, and two sullen, menacing gray eyes which glared at me from under tufted and sandy brows. A high bald head had a small velvet smoking-cap poised coquettishly upon one side of its pink curve. The skull was of enormous capacity, and yet as I looked down I saw to my amazement that the figure of the man was small and frail, twisted in the shoulders and back like one who has suffered from rickets in his childhood.

"What's this?" he cried in a high, screaming voice. "What is the meaning of this intrusion? Didn't I send you word that I would see you to-morrow morning?"

"I am sorry," said I, "but the matter cannot be delayed. Mr. Sherlock Holmes--"

The mention of my friend's name had an extraordinary effect upon the little man. The look of anger passed in an instant from his face. His features became tense and alert.

"Have you come from Holmes?" he asked.

"I have just left him."

"What about Holmes? How is he?"

"He is desperately ill. That is why I have come."

The man motioned me to a chair, and turned to resume his own. As he did so I caught a glimpse of his face in the mirror over the mantelpiece. I could have sworn that it was set in a malicious and abominable smile. Yet I persuaded myself that it must have been some nervous contraction which I had surprised, for he turned to me an instant later with genuine concern upon his features.

"I am sorry to hear this," said he. "I only know Mr. Holmes through some business dealings which we have had, but I have every respect for his talents and his character. He is an amateur of crime, as I am of disease. For him the villain, for me the microbe. There are my prisons," he continued, pointing to a row of bottles and jars which stood upon a side table. "Among those gelatine cultivations some of the very worst offenders in the world are now doing time."

"It was on account of your special knowledge that Mr. Holmes desired to see you. He has a high opinion of you and thought that you were the one man in London who could help him."

The little man started, and the jaunty smoking-cap slid to the floor.

"Why?" he asked. "Why should Mr. Homes think that I could help him in his trouble?"

"Because of your knowledge of Eastern diseases."

"But why should he think that this disease which he has contracted is Eastern?"

"Because, in some professional inquiry, he has been working among Chinese sailors down in the docks."

Mr. Culverton Smith smiled pleasantly and picked up his smoking-cap.

"Oh, that's it--is it?" said he. "I trust the matter is not so grave as you suppose. How long has he been ill?"

"About three days."

"Is he delirious?"

"Occasionally."

"Tut, tut! This sounds serious. It would be inhuman not to answer his call. I very much resent any interruption to my work, Dr. Watson, but this case is certainly exceptional. I will come with you at once."

I remembered Holmes's injunction.

"I have another appointment," said I.

"Very good. I will go alone. I have a note of Mr. Holmes's address. You can rely upon my being there within half an hour at most."

It was with a sinking heart that I reentered Holmes's bedroom. For all that I knew the worst might have happened in my absence. To my enormous relief, he had improved greatly in the interval. His appearance was as ghastly as ever, but all trace of delirium had left him and he spoke in a feeble voice, it is true, but with even more than his usual crispness and lucidity.

"Well, did you see him, Watson?"

"Yes; he is coming."

"Admirable, Watson! Admirable! You are the best of messengers."

"He wished to return with me."

"That would never do, Watson. That would be obviously impossible. Did he ask what ailed me?"

"I told him about the Chinese in the East End."

"Exactly! Well, Watson, you have done all that a good friend could. You can now disappear from the scene."

"I must wait and hear his opinion, Holmes."

"Of course you must. But I have reasons to suppose that this opinion would be very much more frank and valuable if he imagines that we are alone. There is just room behind the head of my bed, Watson."

"My dear Holmes!"

"I fear there is no alternative, Watson. The room does not lend itself to concealment, which is as well, as it is the less likely to arouse suspicion. But just there, Watson, I fancy that it could be done." Suddenly he sat up with a rigid intentness upon his haggard face. "There are the wheels, Watson. Quick, man, if you love me! And don't budge, whatever happens--whatever happens, do you hear? Don't speak! Don't move! Just listen with all your ears." Then in an instant his sudden access of strength departed, and his masterful, purposeful talk droned away into the low, vague murmurings of a semi-delirious man.

From the hiding-place into which I had been so swiftly hustled I heard the footfalls upon the stair, with the opening and the closing of the bedroom door. Then, to my surprise, there came a long silence, broken only by the heavy breathings and gaspings of the sick man. I could imagine that our visitor was standing by the bedside and looking down at the sufferer. At last that strange hush was broken.

"Holmes!" he cried. "Holmes!" in the insistent tone of one who awakens a sleeper. "Can't you hear me, Holmes?" There was a rustling, as if he had shaken the sick man roughly by the shoulder.

"Is that you, Mr. Smith?" Holmes whispered. "I hardly dared hope that you would come."

The other laughed.

"I should imagine not," he said. "And yet, you see, I am here. Coals of fire, Holmes--coals of fire!"

"It is very good of you--very noble of you. I appreciate your special knowledge."

Our visitor sniggered.

"You do. You are, fortunately, the only man in London who does. Do you know what is the matter with you?"

"The same," said Holmes.

"Ah! You recognize the symptoms?"

"Only too well."

"Well, I shouldn't be surprised, Holmes. I shouldn't be surprised if it WERE the same. A bad lookout for you if it is. Poor Victor was a dead man on the fourth day--a strong, hearty young fellow. It was certainly, as you said, very surprising that he should have contracted an out-of-the-way Asiatic disease in the heart of London--a disease, too, of which I had made such a very special study. Singular coincidence, Holmes. Very smart of you to notice it, but rather uncharitable to suggest that it was cause and effect."

"I knew that you did it."

"Oh, you did, did you? Well, you couldn't prove it, anyhow. But what do you think of yourself spreading reports about me like that, and then crawling to me for help the moment you are in trouble? What sort of a game is that--eh?"

I heard the rasping, laboured breathing of the sick man. "Give me the water!" he gasped.

"You're precious near your end, my friend, but I don't want you to go till I have had a word with you. That's why I give you water. There, don't slop it about! That's right. Can you understand what I say?"

Holmes groaned.

"Do what you can for me. Let bygones be bygones," he whispered. "I'll put the words out of my head--I swear I will. Only cure me, and I'll forget it."

"Forget what?"

"Well, about Victor Savage's death. You as good as admitted just now that you had done it. I'll forget it."

"You can forget it or remember it, just as you like. I don't see you in the witnessbox. Quite another shaped box, my good Holmes, I assure you. It matters nothing to me that you should know how my nephew died. It's not him we are talking about. It's you."

"Yes, yes."

"The fellow who came for me--I've forgotten his name--said that you contracted it down in the East End among the sailors."

"I could only account for it so."

"You are proud of your brains, Holmes, are you not? Think yourself smart, don't you? You came across someone who was smarter this time. Now cast your mind back, Holmes. Can you think of no other way you could have got this thing?"

"I can't think. My mind is gone. For heaven's sake help me!"

"Yes, I will help you. I'll help you to understand just where you are and how you got there. I'd like you to know before you die."

"Give me something to ease my pain."

"Painful, is it? Yes, the coolies used to do some squealing towards the end. Takes you as cramp, I fancy."

"Yes, yes; it is cramp."

"Well, you can hear what I say, anyhow. Listen now! Can you remember any unusual incident in your life just about the time your symptoms began?"

"No, no; nothing."

"Think again."

"I'm too ill to think."

"Well, then, I'll help you. Did anything come by post?"

"By post?"

"A box by chance?"

"I'm fainting--I'm gone!"

"Listen, Holmes!" There was a sound as if he was shaking the dying man, and it was all that I could do to hold myself quiet in my hiding-place. "You must hear me. You SHALL hear me. Do you remember a box--an ivory box? It came on Wednesday. You opened it--do you remember?"

"Yes, yes, I opened it. There was a sharp spring inside it. Some joke--"

"It was no joke, as you will find to your cost. You fool, you would have it and you have got it. Who asked you to cross my path? If you had left me alone I would not have hurt you."

"I remember," Holmes gasped. "The spring! It drew blood. This box--this on the table."

"The very one, by George! And it may as well leave the room in my pocket. There goes your last shred of evidence. But you have the truth now, Holmes, and you can die with the knowledge that I killed you. You knew too much of the fate of Victor Savage, so I have sent you to share it. You are very near your end, Holmes. I will sit here and I will watch you die."

Holmes's voice had sunk to an almost inaudible whisper.

"What is that?" said Smith. "Turn up the gas? Ah, the shadows begin to fall, do they? Yes, I will turn it up, that I may see you the better." He crossed the room and the light suddenly brightened. "Is there any other little service that I can do you, my friend?"

"A match and a cigarette."

I nearly called out in my joy and my amazement. He was speaking in his natural voice--a little weak, perhaps, but the very voice I knew. There was a long pause, and I felt that Culverton Smith was standing in silent amazement looking down at his companion.

"What's the meaning of this?" I heard him say at last in a dry, rasping tone.

"The best way of successfully acting a part is to be it," said Holmes. "I give you my word that for three days I have tasted neither food nor drink until you were good enough to pour me out that glass of water. But it is the tobacco which I find most irksome. Ah, here ARE some cigarettes." I heard the striking of a match. "That is very much better. Halloa! halloa! Do I hear the step of a friend?"

There were footfalls outside, the door opened, and Inspector Morton appeared.

"All is in order and this is your man," said Holmes.

The officer gave the usual cautions.

"I arrest you on the charge of the murder of one Victor Savage," he concluded.

"And you might add of the attempted murder of one Sherlock Holmes," remarked my friend with a chuckle. "To save an invalid trouble, Inspector, Mr. Culverton Smith was good enough to give our signal by turning up the gas. By the way, the prisoner has a small box in the right-hand pocket of his coat which it would be as well to remove. Thank you. I would handle it gingerly if I were you. Put it down here. It may play its part in the trial."

There was a sudden rush and a scuffle, followed by the clash of iron and a cry of pain.

"You'll only get yourself hurt," said the inspector. "Stand still, will you?" There was the click of the closing handcuffs.

"A nice trap!" cried the high, snarling voice. "It will bring YOU into the dock, Holmes, not me. He asked me to come here to cure him. I was sorry for him and I came. Now he will pretend, no doubt, that I have said anything which he may invent which will corroborate his insane suspicions. You can lie as you like, Holmes. My word is always as good as yours."

"Good heavens!" cried Holmes. "I had totally forgotten him. My dear Watson, I owe you a thousand apologies. To think that I should have overlooked you! I need not introduce you to Mr. Culverton Smith, since I understand that you met somewhat earlier in the evening. Have you the cab below? I will follow you when I am dressed, for I may be of some use at the station.

"I never needed it more," said Holmes as he refreshed himself with a glass of claret and some biscuits in the intervals of his toilet. "However, as you know, my habits are irregular, and such a feat means less to me than to most men. It was very essential that I should impress Mrs. Hudson with the reality of my condition, since she was to convey it to you, and you in turn to him. You won't be offended, Watson? You will realize that among your many talents dissimulation finds no place, and that if you had shared my secret you would never have been able to impress Smith with the urgent necessity of his presence, which was the vital point of the whole scheme. Knowing his vindictive nature, I was perfectly certain that he would come to look upon his handiwork."

"But your appearance, Holmes--your ghastly face?"

"Three days of absolute fast does not improve one's beauty, Watson. For the rest, there is nothing which a sponge may not cure. With vaseline upon one's forehead, belladonna in one's eyes, rouge over the cheek-bones, and crusts of beeswax round one's lips, a very satisfying effect can be produced. Malingering is a subject upon which I have sometimes thought of writing a monograph. A little occasional talk about half-crowns, oysters, or any other extraneous subject produces a pleasing effect of delirium."

"But why would you not let me near you, since there was in truth no infection?"

"Can you ask, my dear Watson? Do you imagine that I have no respect for your medical talents? Could I fancy that your astute judgment would pass a dying man who, however weak, had no rise of pulse or temperature? At four yards, I could deceive you. If I failed to do so, who would bring my Smith within my grasp? No, Watson, I would not touch that box. You can just see if you look at it sideways where the sharp spring like a viper's tooth emerges as you open it. I dare say it was by some such device that poor Savage, who stood between this monster and a reversion, was done to death. My correspondence, however, is, as you know, a varied one, and I am somewhat upon my guard against any packages which reach me. It was clear to me, however, that by pretending that he had really succeeded in his design I might surprise a confession. That pretence I have carried out with the thoroughness of the true artist. Thank you, Watson, you must help me on with my coat. When we have finished at the police-station I think that something nutritious at Simpson's would not be out of place."

www.sherlockholmesmystery.com

Made in the USA
Monee, IL
05 August 2021

75021661R00118